BLOOD WOLF

HELEN HARDT VINTAGE COLLECTION

HELEN HARDT

HARDT & SONS

BLOOD WOLF
HH VINTAGE COLLECTION

Helen Hardt

HS
HARDT & SONS ♥

This book is an original publication of Helen Hardt

This is a work of fiction. Names, characters, places, and incidents either are the product of the author's imagination or are used fictitiously, and any resemblance to actual persons, living or dead, business establishments, events, or locales is entirely coincidental. The publisher does not assume any responsibility for third-party websites or their content.

Copyright © 2022 Helen Hardt, LLC dba Hardt & Sons
Cover Design: Helen Hardt

Print ISBN: 978-1-952841-12-5

All Rights Reserved

No part of this book may be reproduced, scanned, or distributed in any printed or electronic format without permission. Please do not participate in or encourage piracy of copyrighted materials in violation of the author's rights. Purchase only authorized editions.

PRINTED IN THE UNITED STATES OF AMERICA

HS
HARDT & SONS

For Dan McCune, who loved this story when he first read it ages ago.

ALSO BY HELEN HARDT

Follow Me Series:

Follow Me Darkly

Follow Me Under

Follow Me Always

Darkly

Wolfes of Manhattan

Rebel

Recluse

Runaway

Rake

Reckoning

Billionaire Island (Wolfes continuation)

Escape

Gems of Wolfe Island (Wolfes continuation)

Moonstone

Raven

Garnet

Buck (coming soon)

Steel Brothers Saga:

Trilogy One—Talon and Jade

Craving

Obsession

Possession

Trilogy Two—Jonah and Melanie

Melt

Burn

Surrender

Trilogy Three—Ryan and Ruby

Shattered

Twisted

Unraveled

Trilogy Four—Bryce and Marjorie

Breathless

Ravenous

Insatiable

Trilogy Five—Brad and Daphne

Fate

Legacy

Descent

Trilogy Six—Dale and Ashley

Awakened

Cherished

Freed

Trilogy Seven—Donny and Callie

Spark

Flame

Blaze

Trilogy Eight—Brock and Rory (coming soon)

Smolder

Flare

Scorch

Blood Bond Saga:

Unchained

Unhinged

Undaunted

Unmasked

Undefeated

Sex and the Season:

Lily and the Duke

Rose in Bloom

Lady Alexandra's Lover

Sophie's Voice

Temptation Saga:

Tempting Dusty

Teasing Annie

Taking Catie

Taming Angelina

Treasuring Amber

Trusting Sydney

Tantalizing Maria

Standalone Novels and Novellas

Reunited

Misadventures:

Misadventures of a Good Wife (with Meredith Wild)

Misadventures with a Rockstar

The Cougar Chronicles:

The Cowboy and the Cougar

Calendar Boy

Daughters of the Prairie:

The Outlaw's Angel

Lessons of the Heart

Song of the Raven

Collections:

Destination Desire

Her Two Lovers

Non-Fiction:

got style?

PRAISE FOR HELEN HARDT

WOLFES OF MANHATTAN

"It's hot, it's intense, and the plot starts off thick and had me completely spellbound from page one."
    ~**The Sassy Nerd Blog**

"Helen Hardt...is a master at her craft."
    ~**K. Ogburn, Amazon**

"Move over Steel brothers... Rock is *everything!*"
    ~**Barbara Conklin-Jaros, Amazon**

"Helen has done it again. She winds you up and weaves a web of intrigue."
    ~**Vicki Smith, Amazon**

FOLLOW ME SERIES

"Hardt spins erotic gold..."

~*Publishers Weekly*

"22 Best Erotic Novels to Read"
~*Marie Claire* **Magazine**

"Intensely erotic and wildly emotional..."
~*New York Times* **bestselling author Lisa Renee Jones**

"With an edgy, enigmatic hero and loads of sexual tension, Helen Hardt's fast-paced Follow Me Darkly had me turning pages late into the night!"
~*New York Times* **bestselling author J. Kenner**

"Christian, Gideon, and now...Braden Black."
~**Books, Wine, and Besties**

"A tour de force where the reader will be pulled in as if they're being seduced by Braden Black, taken for a wild ride, and left wanting more."
~*USA Today* **Bestselling Author Julie Morgan**

"Hot. Sexy. Intriguing. Page-Turner. Helen Hardt checks all the boxes with *Follow Me Darkly!*"
~**International Bestselling Author Victoria Blue**

STEEL BROTHERS SAGA

"*Craving* is the jaw-dropping book you *need* to read!"
~*New York Times* **bestselling author Lisa Renee Jones**

"Completely raw and addictive."
~#1 *New York Times* **bestselling author Meredith Wild**

"Talon has hit my top five list...up there next to Jamie Fraser and Gideon Cross."
~USA Today bestselling author Angel Payne

"Talon and Jade's instant chemistry heats up the pages..."
~RT Book Reviews

"Sorry Christian and Gideon, there's a new heartthrob for you to contend with. Meet Talon. Talon Steel."
~Booktopia

"Such a beautiful torment—the waiting, the anticipation, the relief that only comes briefly before more questions arise, and the wait begins again... Check. Mate. Ms. Hardt..."
~Bare Naked Words

"Made my heart stop in my chest. Helen has given us such a heartbreakingly beautiful series."
~Tina, Bookalicious Babes

BLOOD BOND SAGA

"An enthralling and rousing vampire tale that will leave readers waiting for the sequel."
~Kirkus Reviews

"Dangerous and sexy. A new favorite!"
~*New York Times* bestselling author Alyssa Day

"A dark, intoxicating tale."
~Library Journal

"Helen dives into the paranormal world of vampires and makes it her own."

~**Tina, Bookalicious Babes**

"Throw out everything you know about vampires—except for that blood thirst we all love and lust after in these stunning heroes—and expect to be swept up in a sensual story that twists and turns in so many wonderfully jaw-dropping ways."

~**Angel Payne,** *USA Today* **bestselling author**

AUTHOR'S NOTE

Welcome to the Helen Hardt Vintage Collection! These are the back list of my back list—stories that I wrote at the beginning of my career that were never published.

Except this one *was* published.

Blood Wolf was published by The Wild Rose Press in an anthology called *Got Wolf* in 2009 as a result of my winning a wolf shifter writing contest sponsored by the publisher. After the rights reverted to me, I published it again in 2013 through the now defunct Musa Publishing.

I think it sold around five copies total.

I'm not kidding.

Reviews were excellent, except for one that stated (and I'm paraphrasing), "Damian is aggressive, domineering, and just a hair short of insane."

Yeah, that reviewer got my wolf shifter hero. Exactly what I was going for.

I didn't save that one, obviously, but I did save these two:
One of the best books I've read this year.
—Margo Arthur, The Romance Studio

This story was a treat, especially considering the subject matter. It's not uncommon to hear stories of alpha men who meet "the one," instantly glom onto their destined mates, and insist on claiming and protecting him. Ms. Hardt's delivery of this theme, however, is quite unique—particularly the socially awkward nature of an independent woman attempting to interact with the populace as she's chased around by an alpha male. It was both hilarious and highly believable... The side story of Isabella and Rex was intriguing as well. I hope these two have a story in the near future.

—Bitten by Books

My original plan was a four book series. The second book was to be *Blood Witch* and would focus on Rex and Isabella. But when Musa Publishing ceased operations in 2014 and my rights to *Blood Wolf* reverted once more, I put it on the back burner to focus on other projects.

Now it's time to bring it out again. I hope you enjoy Damian and Suzanne's story!

PROLOGUE

The wolf howled, scraping his paws against the bulwark of his prison. He hungered for food, for blood. For the hunt. His claws were dulled from pawing at the gray stone walls that surrounded him. Sometimes he scratched so hard, the sharp nails broke off and bled. Consumed by the need to escape, to hunt, to kill, he felt no pain. His rage darkened and grew stronger as his yelps became louder and more shrill.

The coppery aroma of his own blood fueled his lust for the hunt. His stomach rumbled. He bared his jagged, pointy teeth, growled again, and paced around the inside of his rock dungeon. In his head, rabbits, foxes, humans lay, all dead at his feet, their flesh ripped open by his cuspids.

He lowered his lupine snout to the ground and sniffed. Food was out there. Waiting for him. He picked up the earthy scent of the older human—the one who was kind to him. The aged man was near, somewhere close behind the animal's cage. If the man were to open the door, the wolf would kill him without remorse.

In the barred window high above him, the full moon cast a luminous ray of light upon the floor. The wolf jumped against the stone door with a frenzied howl. He smelled the human's iron-laced blood, heard his heart beating, his lungs expanding with air.

Muscle.

Bones.

Blood.

Meat.

The wolf turned and regarded a pile of splintered remnants, all that was left of the meager meal the human had left for him. The dead meat had sated his stomach hunger, but not his bloodlust. He wanted to hunt.

He *needed* to hunt.

To kill.

He licked his bleeding paws and then continued to sniff, picking up a new scent.

Musky.

Yeasty.

Female.

His cock grew hard. Harder than it had ever been. Gone was the desire to hunt, to kill, to consume the mangled raw flesh of his victim.

He wanted to copulate, spread his seed.

Now.

He threw his muscular body against the bolted stone door, yelping and howling louder than before. Again he pounded, bruising and bloodying himself, his thick black fur falling to the ground in clumps.

He continued until he collapsed from exhaustion, his body weakened, his unsated lust consuming him. He dreamed of mounting his mate, of thrusting himself into her.

Of claiming her.

1

Dumped.

Unceremoniously dumped by Wade Stallworth at the coffee shop across the street from her office.

So sorry. Someone else. Never expected this. A woman at the office. Soul mates. Still friends?

Suzanne had numbly nodded, murmured something about understanding, and walked back to her office. There she had sat, staring at the rock he had given her over a year ago. Why hadn't he asked her to return it? She supposed the expense of such a bauble meant nothing to him.

Suzanne looked at her cousin, Isabella, who was driving the rented economy car down the dark and winding Scottish country road. Isabella was a self-proclaimed witch, but she wanted no part of black magic, as she called it. No help there. Suzanne didn't believe in any of that stuff anyway. Still, the thought of Wade ending up with a case of blistering jock rash made her feel slightly better, if only for a second.

But the next second, the tears came again. Only a few,

accompanied by quiet sobs. Isabella reached over and patted Suzanne's thigh.

"God, I'm sorry, Bell. Here I go again."

"It's okay, Suzie. It's going to take a while. You were with Wade for years."

Suzanne nodded and wiped her nose. "You know, he never said I was beautiful. The man I marry should think I'm beautiful, shouldn't he?"

"Of course he should," Isabella said, "and you are."

But Suzanne had never thought so. Instead of dark gray eyes, she had always wanted blue. And instead of her boring brown hair, she coveted Isabella's blondness. Suzanne's curves and long oval face paled in comparison to her cousin's lithe build. Isabella, at five feet six and a half inches, was the perfect height and made Suzanne feel like an Amazon at five feet nine.

She choked back another sob. "I don't want to ruin this trip for you."

Suzanne had taken a leave of absence from her law firm to accompany Isabella to northern Scotland. Isabella's grandmother, whom she barely knew, had died recently and left her only grandchild a small castle outside a remote little village called Padraig. Suzanne loved all things Highland and Gaelic. But the trip that should have been a dream come true was tainted by Isabella's grandmother's death and Suzanne's own recent dumping.

"Don't be silly." Isabella rubbed Suzanne's thigh again. "I want you here. I wouldn't have asked you otherwise."

Suzanne sighed. Isabella had been her rock since the Wade debacle. Suzanne was glad to be out of Denver, out of the whole freaking United States. Here in Scotland, Wade could become part of her past, and perhaps she could think about her future—her law practice, her desire for a home and children.

A future without Wade.

"Just look at that moon, Suze," Isabella said. "There's incredible lunar energy here. I can't wait to get to the castle. I want to do my *Esbat* before midnight."

"Bell, midnight has no meaning here. I mean, we're still on Mountain Standard Time. Midnight won't hit us for about eight hours yet." Suzanne sniffed away her sobs. "What is midnight, anyway? When you think about it, it's always midnight somewhere, isn't it? And what if you go into a different time zone? Does that change your *Esbat* thingie?"

"You are such a freaking lawyer, Suzanne," Isabella said. "Do you always have to be so analytical?"

A small giggle escaped Suzanne's constricted throat.

"Ha! I made you laugh." Isabella punched Suzanne's arm. "I'll tolerate your pontificating if the end result is your laughter."

Suzanne smiled at her pretty cousin. "We must be nearly there, Bell. How much farther, do you think?"

"Not too much. I need to make a left turn up ahead. In fact, that's probably the castle over there." She pointed.

Suzanne squinted. Even in the light of the full moon, the gray granite of the castle was difficult to make out. It looked old and dreary. A bit of light glowed out from the stone, but nothing more indicated that anyone lived there.

"Don't we have to drive through Padraig?"

Isabella shook her head. "My grandmother left explicit instructions with her attorneys. We're to take these small roads to the castle. In fact, she was adamant that we *not* drive through Padraig."

"Why?"

"Don't ask me. It's probably one of those funky little towns where you can't get there from here, you know what I mean? The roads probably take you thirty miles out of your way."

"It can't be any farther out of our way than these tiny roads are." Suzanne glanced at her watch. *Ten thirty.* "I feel like we've been driving forever."

"Yeah, I know what you mean," Isabella agreed, making the final turn. "But there's the castle, straight ahead."

"Finally." Suzanne yawned. "I'm so exhausted. I feel like I've been awake for twenty-four hours."

"You have been."

"Yeah, I know. You can't still be thinking about doing your ritual tonight, can you? Don't you want to just fall into bed?"

"No way. By tomorrow, the moon will be waning, and I may never experience lunar energy of this magnitude again in my lifetime," Isabella said. "I will be out there under it, skyclad. In fact, I was hoping you would do me the tiniest favor?"

Suzanne groaned. "No, Bell. No way."

"Please, Suze? I really need your feminine energy if I'm going to draw down the moon tonight."

"I'm exhausted!"

"I know, but please? You're the only woman around. I'll never ask you for another thin. I swear it."

"Oh, you will too. We both know it, so quit making that promise."

Isabella giggled. "You know me so well. Come on. I know you don't believe the way I do, but trust me, I need your presence tonight. It's nice and warm out. And the moon is amazing. You might even enjoy it."

Right. "Do I have to be naked?"

"Well, it helps the energy, yeah."

"Christ."

As Isabella pulled the VW into the long gravel driveway of the castle, Suzanne made a mental note to have her cousin replace it with concrete or asphalt. This was the twenty-first century after all. They could at least have modern conveniences. She sighed as she imagined the type of plumbing they might encounter.

"Who lives here again?" Suzanne asked as they grabbed their suitcases out of the small trunk.

"Just the caretaker, Dougal something, and his son. The attorneys said they've been here for years, taking care of the place for my grandmother."

"Was there any money in her bequest? Surely she can't expect you to take care of such an old place without any capital."

"A little. About fifty thousand pounds."

"Not a lot, but all in all, not a bad nest egg."

"No, but...oh, look."

An older man opened the front door, holding a candle.

"Miss Knight?"

"Yes," Isabella said. "I'm Isabella Knight, and this is my cousin, Suzanne Wood."

The man came toward them and took the suitcase from Isabella's hand. He gave his candle to Isabella and reached for Suzanne's suitcase. "I'm Dougal MacGowan, the caretaker. I'll take these for you."

"Thank you," Isabella said.

"Your grandmother often spoke of you. Damian and I were so sorry when she passed on. She was like a light around here."

"Spoke of me?"

"Aye."

"But we never met."

"I know. But you were her only kin. She had some photos of you when you were a bairn. Your mother must have sent them before she passed on. She used to talk of meeting you. Damian and I never grew tired of her stories."

"Damian?"

"My son. Come in," he said. "I've fixed up your grandmother's room for you. And you," he said to Suzanne, "can use Damian's room. It's the nicest next to Merlina's. He's out tonight, so he won't mind."

"That's not necessary," Suzanne said. "Any guest room will be fine."

"I won't hear of it. Damian can take a different room when he returns. You're kin to Miss Knight. The room should be yours."

"Please. I can't take his room away. Especially when he isn't even here."

"Oh, he'd insist," the man said. "I cleaned it and changed the bedding today and moved his things to a vacant chamber."

"But—"

"I won't take no for an answer, young lady."

Suzanne, too fatigued to argue, muttered, "Fine, fine. Just lead me to the nearest bed."

"Suze," Isabella began.

"Yes, I know, you need me. Don't worry. I'm just going to lie down for a few minutes."

When they entered the castle, Dougal lit another candle, and his features became more apparent. He was a handsome older gentleman with grayish blond hair and green eyes. He didn't move toward a light switch.

"Please tell me we have electricity here," Isabella said.

"I'm afraid not. Merlina never wanted to install it."

"Well, that's first on my list. What about indoor plumbing?"

"That we have," Dougal said. "Damian and I finally convinced her to install running water five years ago. She fought us. Said it would destroy the castle's character. But in the end, she decided it would be easier for her, and it was."

"Thank God," Suzanne said.

"Believe me, we did." Dougal chuckled. "Each chamber has its own bathroom. In fact, once Merlina decided to do it, she did it pure dead brilliant. I think you'll both be pleased."

Suzanne wasn't able to see much of the interior of the castle. Dougal led her and Isabella up a long narrow staircase and down a hall to several closed doors.

"Here you are, Miss Wood." He opened the door, set her suitcase by the bed, and lit several lamps, which cast a soft veil of light over what turned out to be a very large chamber. "I hope this will suit you."

"My, it's lovely," Suzanne said. "And so large."

"That door over there leads to your bathroom," he said. "I'll leave you to get settled in. Come, Miss Knight."

Suzanne walked to the large, canopied bed covered with a silky comforter and sat. Sighing, she swung her legs up, lay down, and allowed the softness to comfort her tired body. *Oh, this will work out just fine. Damian be damned.* She wasn't giving up this room, or this bed.

She didn't realize she had fallen asleep until a knock woke her.

"It's me, Suze," Isabella's voice said. "It's time."

"Shit," Suzanne said to herself. "Coming!"

She opened the door, and there stood Isabella, clad in a satin robe. "You're not ready."

"Sorry. I got on the bed, and the rest is history."

"Well, come on." Isabella walked into the room, picked up Suzanne's suitcase, tossed it on the bed, and opened it. "Where's your robe?"

"Hold on, I'll find it." Suzanne pawed around and pulled out a fuzzy pink garment.

"Okay, second thing, after we install electricity, is to get you a new robe."

"Very funny."

"All right. Get undressed."

Suzanne complied quickly, put on her robe, and followed Isabella down the stairs and out a back door of the castle. They stood in an enchanting courtyard flanked by statues of glimmering wolves and fairies illuminated by the light of the full moon. Suzanne drew in a deep breath. The landscaping was beautiful. She could hardly wait to see it in the daylight.

"Come on." Isabella pulled her arm. "I'm going to cast my circle here." She gestured to an open area surrounded by young trees and gardens. "I feel lots of positive energy."

"What do I do?"

"Just stand here, inside the circle, until it's cast. Then I'll show you how to draw down the moon."

Suzanne started walking, but Isabella shook her head.

"Lose the robe, Suze."

"Oh, right." She untied the sash. "What if Dougal can see us?"

"So what?"

"Bell—"

"He already went to bed, Suze."

"God."

"Just do it. You promised."

Dear God. Suzanne ripped her robe from her body and tossed it onto the soft grass. "Now what?"

"Step inside the circle, where I showed you."

Suzanne stood still as Isabella walked in a circle, naked, and poured salt from a glass container while she chanted. Then she moved to the center of the circle, next to Suzanne.

"I want you to visualize the energy of the Goddess coming from the moon. Think of the color white, for the maiden aspect, because you and I are maidens. Imagine a veil of white energy radiating from the moon and into your body."

Suzanne closed her eyes.

"Feel the warmth of the Goddess enter your body, your spirit." Isabella took Suzanne's hands into hers.

Suzanne kept her eyes closed as the warm energy from Isabella's fingers seeped into her own. Slowly, she and Isabella walked in a circle and raised their arms toward the moon. Suzanne saw the white energy in her mind, but she didn't expect to feel anything. So she was more than a little surprised when the jolt of power entered her body, warming her and sending tingles through her veins.

As she danced to the moon goddess, Suzanne's heart sang. The sounds of the night enshrouded her—crickets chirping, the night breeze blowing gently, and somewhere nearby, a wolf howling.

2

The wolf, his body battered and weak, roared within the stone dungeon. He looked toward the barred window above him and scented two females on the ground, moving in time with the midsummer wind. Their musky aroma drifted upward.

His cock hardened. He yelped and howled, flinging himself against the rocky wall once more. The bloody scabs on his pelt opened and oozed, leaving sticky red streaks on the gray stone. He had but one primal thought in his animal mind—to escape this prison and mate, to spill his seed into a warm female body.

He forced his wails across the winds, down into the courtyard below.

3

Suzanne awoke after ten p.m. She hadn't meant to sleep so long. She would never conquer her jet lag if she didn't force herself to wake after eight hours. Isabella hadn't awakened her, nor had Dougal. And now, darkness clouded the night.

She lit several lamps and went to her bathroom to take a shower. Finally clean and fresh after three days, she dressed in a pair of jeans and a turquoise tank top. She grabbed a candle and headed downstairs to find something to eat. She pawed through the large pantry, but found only crackers, carrots, and onions.

Hadn't Dougal thought to lay in supplies before she and Isabella arrived? Then again, what could she expect from a medieval castle that lacked refrigeration?

She walked briskly back to her room and found her map of Padraig and the surrounding area, along with her set of keys to the rented car. She needed some real food. Surely there would be a fast food place somewhere in town. She'd seen them all over London and Edinburgh. Even a scone from a coffee shop sounded good.

She blew out the candle, left it on a table beside the main door, and stepped into the warm summer night. How very strange to emerge into total darkness. Such was the case with no outdoor lighting. Only the waning moon cast a gossamer curtain against the castle grounds. Tomorrow, she'd talk to Dougal about lighting some flaming torches or something, at least until everyone was in bed. She felt her way to the small vehicle and let herself in. She turned the ignition and flicked on the headlights.

Sight! A marvelous invention.

She clicked on the reading lamp and studied the map. The castle didn't seem too far away from the little village after all. Maybe ten miles or so. A couple of turns and she'd be there.

She expected a quaint little Highland town.

What she got surprised her. As she approached the small village of Padraig, surreal neon lights nearly blinded her. Was this freaking Vegas in Scotland? Okay, it wasn't exactly the strip—Padraig was a tiny village, after all—but she didn't expect the carousing nightlife she found. Thrilled at the prospect of finding something better than a fast food burger to eat, she parked at a cute little café and walked inside.

"Hello there," a plump waitress called. "Welcome to Café Oxter. Just sit anywhere you want. I'll be right with you."

Suzanne smiled and settled into a corner booth, out of the way.

"I'm Gwennie," the waitress said and handed her a menu. "You new around here?"

"Yeah. I just got in yesterday."

"American, are you?"

"My accent give me away?" Suzanne smiled.

"That and the way you're dressed. Hey—" She lowered her voice. "Are you out here alone?"

"Yeah."

"Oh."

"Is there a problem?"

"No. No." Gwennie's voice sounded edgy. It cracked a little, and her gaze darted toward the door. "Not yet, anyway."

"Look, I'm famished, so—"

"Of course, dearie. What'll it be?"

"I would absolutely love a cup of cock-a-leekie, and a cheeseburger, medium rare, with fries."

Gwennie laughed. "You're American, all right. No one but a yank would order cock-a-leekie with a burger."

"Hey, it sounds good. I haven't had a decent meal in over twenty-four hours."

"I understand. What to drink?"

"What the hell," Suzanne said. "Bring me a pint of Guinness."

"You're in Scotland, not Ireland, dearie."

"Does that mean you don't have Guinness?"

Gwennie let out a gutsy laugh. "Aye, we have Guinness. I'll fetch it for you."

The café was oddly busy for eleven on a Wednesday evening. When Gwennie arrived with her Guinness, Suzanne asked, "Is it always this hopping during the week?"

"Hopping?"

"You know, busy?"

"We have quite a night life here in Padraig. What brings you here, anyway?"

"My cousin inherited the little stone castle to the north."

"Merlina O'Day's place?"

Suzanne nodded. "Isabella hardly knew her. We just got in late last night. I woke up and there was nothing to eat in the kitchen, so I got in the car, and here I am."

"Dearie, there's something you should know about Padraig—"

Gwennie stopped in mid-sentence as several men entered the café. A large blond man caught Suzanne's eye.

"Christ a'mighty. Your meal'll be out in a minute. Excuse me." Gwennie walked away briskly and turned to the new arrivals. "Sit down and behave yourselves, or by God, I'll throw you out of here."

Suzanne shifted in her seat. The blond man eyed her. Her pulse quickened, and shivers rippled up her arms. *Get out of here.* Every instinct inside her screamed at her to leave. She lifted her purse and prepared to stand, when Gwennie came back carrying her bowl of soup and plate of food. Hell, she *was* starving.

She finished her soup and had taken three bites of her burger, when a striking black-haired man sat down across from her. "Medium rare, eh? Me, I prefer them bloody."

"Excuse me?" Suzanne stared into the man's icy blue eyes. Her stomach lurched. Something was not right here. *I should have left when I had the chance.*

"Bloody rare. That's the only way to eat beef of any kind."

"That's an E. coli nightmare."

"You're new here."

"Yes, and I don't recall asking for company."

The man laughed, exposing very white, straight teeth. "I'm Rex. Rex Donnelly."

"Fascinating."

"Not a friendly sort, are you?"

"I've suddenly lost my appetite." Suzanne rose and

covered her unfinished meal with her napkin. She reached into her purse, pulled out a few notes, and laid them on the table. "Tell Gwennie to keep the change."

She stomped out of the café into the warm summer night. She checked her watch. Nearly midnight. What had she been thinking, coming out after dark in an unfamiliar town?

"A fine lass like yourself shouldn't be wandering around at night."

Her arm jerked backward as her neck prickled. She turned to face Rex Donnelly.

"Let me walk you to your ride."

"No thank you. I'm perfectly capable—"

"I insist." He pulled her into the shadows and behind the building.

"My car is out front," Suzanne said.

"Just a little detour. You won't be harmed."

"Please, I really just want to—"

Suzanne gasped as Rex pushed her into a trio of men waiting behind the café.

"Here you are," Rex said. "Fresh. American, no less. Take only a taste. You know the rules."

He disappeared into the shadows.

Suzanne's heart pounded as the three men eyed her. Their lascivious gazes seemed to melt through her clothes. The big blond from the café stepped forward and cupped her cheek in one large, calloused hand.

"Mighty pretty," he said.

Dear God, no.

"What do you want? I don't have any money."

"It's not your money we're after, lass," the second man said. His black eyes burnt holes in Suzanne's skin.

"God, please don't hurt me." Her heart hammered. "I-I won't tell anyone about this. I swear I won't."

"You're right about that," the third man said. His long nutmeg hair rustled in the night breeze. "You won't remember it." He stepped forward, pulled a strap of Suzanne's tank down over her shoulder so it draped along her upper arm, and grabbed her breast roughly, pinching the nipple. "She's stacked mighty nice."

Suzanne's breath came in rapid pants, and her heart stampeded.

God, please let it happen quickly. Quickly, and with minimal pain.

The blond stepped forward. His pale hair was caught in a low ponytail, and a few wisps hung around his harsh face.

Lord, he'd be handsome if he weren't so evil.

His green eyes smoked as he gazed into Suzanne's. "We'll be quick, lass. I promise you that."

Suzanne squeezed her eyes shut, and something grazed her neck. *Lips? No. It felt sharp.* Something scraped against her skin.

She opened her mouth and let out a piercing scream. "Help me! Someone help me! Please!"

4

Suddenly, a rumble emerged from the darkness. Suzanne opened her eyes only slightly to see a dark figure step forward. Briskly, he pushed the nutmeg-haired man to the ground and then dispensed with the black-eyed one. Before the blond could harm Suzanne, the tall figure wrenched him from her and slammed his ponytailed head into the brick wall of the café.

Suzanne screamed and sank to the ground, hot tears falling from her eyes. Her stomach clenched, and she doubled over, but then forced her body to straighten, unable to tear her eyes from the man who had rescued her.

"You ever come near her again, and I'll kill you, do you understand me, you bastard?" The stranger's Scottish lilt was deep and husky. Again, he pounded the blond man's head into the wall.

Suzanne watched in horror as blood gushed from the man's ears and mouth. His skull thudded against the reddish stone, and several streams of crimson trickled along the brick.

"Please stop! You'll kill him!"

The stranger turned and stared at her, one arm still holding the blond. The irises of his hazel eyes swirled in the moonlight. He returned his attention to her attacker.

"I won't say it again, you fucking pile of sludge. You stay the hell away from her."

The blond man, miraculously still alive, buried his nose in the stranger's neck and then looked up, and his gaze met Suzanne's.

"*Voldlak*," he said, and fell to the ground.

The stranger knelt in front of Suzanne and gathered her in his arms. "Trust me," he said as he carried her to his motorcycle and placed her on the seat. "You'll have to hold on to me."

He started the engine, and with a few roaring gusts, they rode off.

Petrified, Suzanne clung to the muscular form in front of her. She had never ridden on a motorcycle before, and her fear, combined with the stress of her near rape, caused her to sob uncontrollably. When they finally reached the castle, the man parked the bike and carried Suzanne gently inside and up to her room.

He opened the door, and still holding her, let her feet touch the floor. "I-I don't know how to thank you," she said. "If you hadn't come along when you did—"

"What the hell were you thinking?" His bellow shook the room. "Don't you know better than to go into town alone at night?"

"I-I—"

The man crushed her body to his and buried his face in her neck. "If anything had happened to you..."

"I'm f-fine. Really. Oh God, oh God." Tears fell down her cheeks, their heat burning little trails into her delicate skin.

"You're all right now." He pressed his nose to her neck. "It's over. It's over."

"Th-Thank you."

His Scottish lilt had softened to an almost English accent. He pulled away from her for a moment, and even in the dim light of the candles, she could see he was extraordinarily handsome. Wavy dark brown hair fell to his collar and framed his perfectly sculpted face. His eyes were the color of jade veiled in light cognac.

"*Mo cridhe*, you're beautiful." His eyes grazed over her face and then her body.

"I-I'm a mess."

"Can you smell me?"

Suzanne shook her head, confused. "What?"

"God, I want to fuck you."

She blinked, unable to ascertain whether she had heard him correctly.

"I want to touch you everywhere, *mo cridhe*. I want to bury my face between your legs and make you come again and again, until I'm drowning in your cream. I want to thrust myself so deep inside you that you won't be able to tell where I end and you begin, and then I want to fuck you until you cry for me. I want to absorb you into my body—"

Suzanne pulled away, her skin crawling with invisible bugs. "Oh my God. I just escaped a gangbang. You're not going to...*rape* me are you?"

His eyes softened and looked sad, forlorn. "God no, love. I'd never hurt you."

"Wh-Who are you?"

He walked farther into the room and sat down on the bed. "This is my room."

"You're Dougal's son?"

"Aye. Damian."

"Of course you may have your room back," Suzanne said. "I never felt comfortable taking it. I'll move out tomorrow."

"Don't bother."

"Where will you stay?"

"Here."

Suzanne jerked her head toward him. "You can't be serious."

"I am. I'm staying here with you. I belong with you and you with me. I want your fragrance near me, *you* near me."

Suzanne swallowed, confused by Damian's words. "Look, I appreciate what you did for me tonight. Really I do. But saving my life doesn't give you license to my sexual favors."

"Don't you understand?" Damian stood up and pulled Suzanne into his embrace again. "Don't you feel this? My heart is beating for you. I can't think of anything but you, of getting inside you. Can't you...what's your name, anyway?"

Suzanne rolled her eyes. "All this sexy talk, and you don't even know my name."

"I will in a minute."

"Fine. It's Suzanne."

"Suzanne. Beautiful."

"Damian—" She enjoyed the caress of his name on her lips and tongue.

He grasped her hand and held it to his chest. "Can't you feel it?"

Suzanne trembled as he lowered her hand from his heart to his crotch and pressed her fingers into the stiff ridge beneath his jeans. "I'm hard for you. I've been hard since I first smelled you."

"You *smelled* me? What in the world?" She removed her hand from his arousal and tried to shake free of his grip. He held her hand firmly, though, and roughness scraped her palm. Her eyes widened at the scabs on his fingertips. "My goodness, what happened to you?"

"Nothing."

"That's not nothing. You look like you've been clawing a brick wall. Are you all right?"

"I said it's nothing!"

She shrank away at his harsh tone.

"I'm sorry, *mo cridhe*. Don't back away from me. Please."

Puzzled, Suzanne gazed into his greenish eyes. *Mo cridhe.* My heart, in old Scottish Gaelic. She didn't realize the language was still spoken, but then, Padraig was a small village in the northern Highlands.

Pain and torment filled his eyes, but she also saw kindness and compassion. His gaze burned onto her and inflamed her. Her pulse quickened and tingles rushed over her skin. Between her legs, a flicker of desire sparked. She wanted him.

She slowly inched forward, her knees wobbly, and fell into his embrace. He lowered his head until his lips touched hers.

"Suzanne," he whispered against her mouth, "open for me. Please."

Heady turbulence rushed through her. His voice, even in a whisper, spoke to her soul.

She parted her lips, expecting him to plunge into her mouth, but he entered slowly, cautiously, and took only the smallest taste. She let her tongue touch his, and she shuddered. He tasted of cloves. Cloves and sweet wine. She deepened the kiss. His groan signaled approval.

He thrust his body into hers, and he pushed his arousal against her. Damian trailed his lips from her mouth to her cheek and then to her neck, and he inhaled deeply.

"You taste even better than you smell, *mo cridhe*," he said. "Touch me."

"Wh-What?" Suzanne's voice cracked.

"Touch me. Put your hands on me. Please."

Her arms dangled limply at her sides. *Touch him?* Her nerves tightened in her stomach, and her arms trembled as she slowly raised her hands and grasped his sinewy shoulders.

"Ah, yes, that's it, love." He groaned, and his body quivered beneath her fingertips. He nibbled and sucked at her pulse point. "God, I want you. I have to fuck you. Please."

Suzanne's eyes clouded with lust, her pulse raced. Oh, she wanted him. Sex with him seemed like a terrific idea. At least that's what her body thought, and her mind wasn't far behind. How easy it would be to surrender to him. To this gorgeous enigmatic man who wanted her. What a soothing salve for her shattered ego. In one night, she could reverse the damage Wade had done. So tempting.

But it couldn't happen.

It was unimaginably difficult to break away. Especially when she saw the agony in his smoking eyes.

"Suzanne?"

"Look, I'm sorry, but we just met." *God, you'll never know how truly sorry I am.* "I appreciate what you did for me tonight, and I promise I'll never go to town alone again. But I just can't sleep with you. I don't even know you."

"Aye, you do. You feel the connection. Don't deny it."

Suzanne's skin erupted into tiny bumps. She did feel a connection, and it scared her. "This is insane."

"No, it's not. I can't explain it, love, but I feel it. I've been hard since you came here. I hadn't even met you, yet I knew you were in trouble tonight, and I came for you." He raked his fingers through his mass of dark waves.

A bolt of lightning struck her pussy. He was so gorgeous. "You don't understand. I just got out of a messy relationship. It would be a mistake for me to..." She paused, his words sinking into her mind. "What do you mean you knew I was in trouble?"

"I felt it. I knew exactly where I had to go to find you. I smelled your fear."

"Damian, what is it with you and smell?"

"I don't know. I can't explain it. But I am certain of one thing."

"What?"

"That you're mine."

"Oh." Suzanne sighed as his gaze seemed to penetrate her. She didn't doubt that he believed the truth of his words. This beautiful man said more with his smoldering eyes than most people said with language. She couldn't deny that she felt a bond with him.

But that's textbook, she told herself. *I'm attracted to my savior. Who wouldn't be?*

Damian approached her, took her hand in his, and caressed her palm with his scabbed fingertips. "I don't expect you to understand this when I can't explain it to myself. But there is not a doubt in my mind that you belong with me."

"You don't know anything about me."

"I know your hair is the color of burnt mahogany, and it feels like silk against my skin." He sifted her tresses with his fingers and cupped her cheek. "I know your eyes are like the night fog, with little golden sparks that pierce the thickness around my soul." He ran his thumb across her lower lip. "I know your mouth tastes of wintergreen and fresh blueberries. I know your body feels like heaven pressed to mine. I know your beautiful name fits you. I know there's an idiot somewhere who let you go, but I thank God for his stupidity." He lightly traced the angle of her jaw line. "I know you're mine."

Suzanne quivered. Her nipples tightened and her clit began to pulse. This man was seducing her with mere words. She was close to climaxing already, something she had only managed previously by masturbating. Never with a man.

"I won't force you to lie with me," Damian said, "but I will share this room with you. That's not negotiable. I need to be close to you."

"I can't allow you to stay here. If you want the room—"

"I said it's not negotiable!"

Suzanne jumped as Damian pounded his fist into the adjacent wall.

"I need to be with you. I need your scent near me."

"What you want is impossible." Her voice cracked with nerves. "I refuse to share a bed with a man I just met."

"I will leave you alone, but we *will* share this bed."

He lifted his shirt over his head and threw it over a chair. She gulped in a sharp breath. His chest was golden and beautiful, pure muscle accented by a smattering of black hair. Suzanne instinctively looked away as he began to unbuckle his jeans.

"No." He cupped her face, forcing her gaze onto his. "I need you to look at me. To *see* me."

As if in a trance, Suzanne stared as Damian slowly

removed his shoes, jeans, and boxers. His cock sprang from a curly black nest. Perfectly formed. Beautiful. She resisted the urge to reach for it.

"Now you," he said. "Undress."

"I can't."

"Aye, you can. I need to see you."

She edged away slowly. "I'll just go to the bathroom, and—"

"You'll undress here." He grasped her arm. His touch was forceful, yet gentle. "Don't be afraid. I would never harm you, *mo cridhe*. I swear on my life."

Suzanne shivered as she slowly pulled her tank top over her head. Next, she kicked off her sandals and lowered her jeans, until she stood before Damian in her bra and panties.

"Very beautiful." There was no mistaking the lust in his hazel eyes. "The rest, please."

Her hands shaking, Suzanne reached behind her, unclasped her bra, discarded it, and let her ample breasts fall gently against her chest. Damian sucked in his breath. She hadn't been worried. She knew her boobs were spectacular. But the panties concerned her. Her thick and bushy pubic hair had been a source of contention between her and Wade. He had wanted her to shave and trim it into a neat little strip, but she had always refused.

"Don't be nervous," he said gently, as if sensing her unease.

His words consoled her, and it seemed natural to ease her pink panties over her hips and let them drop to the floor. She stood before him, naked and vulnerable. Her heart nearly stopped as she waited for his appraisal.

He stepped toward her, cupped her breasts, and gently rubbed his calloused thumbs over her nipples. One hand trailed down her belly to her mound. He laced his fingers through the thick hair, his breathing heavy, his cock engorged. "Perfect," he said gruffly. "Perfect, *mo cridhe*."

"Now what?"

He kissed her softly on the cheek. "Now, I hold you next to my body. We share our heat, our intimacy." He brushed his lips over hers. "And we sleep." He lifted her and laid her gently on the bed. He crawled in beside her and cuddled her in his arms.

Suzanne lay still, nestled in the comfort of this mysterious man. The light fleece of his chest tickled her nipples. She felt safe. After what had nearly happened to her, she needed this sense of security. He had saved her, and now he protected her.

She listened to the hypnotic rhythm of his breath and soon fell into slumber beside him.

5

When Suzanne awoke, Damian lay on his side, his hand propping up his head as he stared at her. His smoking eyes scalded her naked flesh.

"Good morning, Suzanne."

"Good morning." The light of dawn streamed through her window and illuminated the fascinating man next to her. He had seemed handsome last night, but now, bathed in the sun's rays, he stole her breath.

Several dark curls fell over his forehead. Suzanne instinctively reached out to smooth them but stopped midway, embarrassed.

Damian clutched her hand and led it to his face. "Don't be afraid."

"I just...your hair is in your eyes." She pushed the offending locks behind his ear. His tresses felt sleek and velvety beneath her fingers. She whisked her hand away.

He smiled and held out his arms to her. "Come to me. Please, *mo cridhe.*"

Her heart lurched, and a flutter surged between her legs.

Oh God, I want him. She glanced at his mouth—such a sensuous full-lipped mouth that promised endless delights—and then into his eyes. The jade irises were swirling again, as they had when he had attacked her assailants.

Odd. Very odd. But arousing.

"Come," he said. "Just a hug. Please."

One hug wouldn't hurt, would it? He was so gorgeous, and that body... She had never seen such a well-formed man. She leaned into his embrace.

"Ah, love," he said, his deep voice husky. "That feels nice."

Damian pulled her close and caressed her shoulders and her back. She reciprocated and ran her hands over the definition of his upper arms and then up his neck and into his beautiful hair.

He buried his nose in her tangled mass of hair and inhaled. "Mmm."

What was this fascination he had with her scent? Suzanne didn't understand, but at the moment, her body ached with the need to touch every part of him. She slid her hands along his neck, over his muscular shoulders, and onto his back. But where she expected more of his smooth skin, raised and jagged bumps met her fingertips.

"Damian?"

"Hmm?"

"What's wrong with your back?" Suzanne pulled away from his embrace and climbed over him to the other side of the bed.

"Oh!" She clasped her hand to her mouth. What she saw was both beautiful and terrible. Deep scratches and oozing scabs knifed through a large tattoo of a black and silver wolf howling at the moon. Despite the mess, Suzanne couldn't help but stare at the tattoo. The wolf's green eyes looked almost...*human*. "What happened to you?"

"It's nothing." Damian turned over, hiding his back from her.

"It most certainly is not nothing," she said. "Who did this to you?"

"It's not your concern."

"Of course it's my concern. If you expect me to share your bed, I expect something in return. I expect your honesty."

"I am being honest. I'm telling you that it's not your concern."

"Are you in pain?"

"No."

"Does this have anything to do with what happened to your hands?"

"Enough! There will be no more talk of this!" He pulled her on top of him and thrust his erection against her body. "I've waited long enough. I'll have you now."

Suzanne shrugged. She couldn't give into his demands, no matter how much her body craved it. "I won't sleep with you. You promised you wouldn't hurt me."

"I have no intention of hurting you. I'll get you ready first."

"No. Please. No!" She scrambled off the bed and into the bathroom and slammed the door behind her. She turned on the faucet to hide her soft sobs, splashed some water on her face, and then looked around for her robe. It wasn't there.

"Suzanne?" Damian's dispirited husky voice cut through the wooden door that separated them.

His agony touched her, but Suzanne didn't answer.

"Love, talk to me."

"I have nothing to say to you."

"I'm sorry. I just want you so badly..." His forehead thunked against the door. "I don't understand what's happening to me."

The anguish in his voice was unmistakable. Despite being terrified he might take her against her will, Suzanne felt an uncontrollable urge to go to him, to comfort him as he had comforted her last night. Her hand levitated over the crystal doorknob for half a minute, and then she grabbed it and turned.

He stood against the wall, naked and beautiful, his ebony-lashed eyes tormented with sorrow. "Forgive me." He held out his arms.

As Suzanne went to him in a haze, she had a sense of watching herself from the ceiling. She saw herself tilt her head and offer him her mouth. He took it gently and wrapped his strong arms around her curvaceous body. He caressed her shoulders, her arms, her back, her buttocks. She watched him kiss her lips, her cheek, her neck and shoulders. As his mouth descended to her breast, she smiled.

But when his tongue touched her nipple, she careened back into her body with full force, and a fiery shock slammed through her.

"Oh my God," she moaned. "Oh, Damian."

"I know, love." He pressed his mouth to her other breast. "I want you, too."

"This is insane. We can't. We shouldn't. *I* shouldn't."

"It'll be okay. I promise." He bent his head and sucked her nipple harder.

She threaded her fingers through his silky hair as her body undulated against him. Nectar slid from her and dripped down the inside of her thighs. Her womb throbbed. As if he could read her mind, Damian reached down to her mound and laced through her thick bush to find the swollen nub. She gasped as he flicked it, rubbed his hand in her wetness, and circled her clit.

"Oh God." Suzanne closed her eyes and leaned back, arching into him. "Oh, God. Oh my God!"

"Come," he said, his voice low and husky. "Come for me, *mo cridhe*."

Suzanne's body burst into flames as throbbing heat enveloped her. Her mons spasmed against his hand. The electric current spread into her legs and belly, to her arms, to her head. Even her eyelids tingled as she panted and thrust against him.

"Damian," she whimpered. "My God, Damian."

He lifted her in his arms, carried her to the bed, and laid her upon the soft mattress. Embarrassed, she turned her head into the pillow.

He gently pulled her face back toward him. "Look at me, Suzanne. Don't force your eyes from mine. We belong together."

She blinked, and a lone tear fell.

"What is it?"

"I—" She gulped. "My fiancé. He never made me feel like that."

Damian's green eyes smoldered. "Then he didn't know how to love you properly."

Words failed Suzanne. She simply nodded. She had no doubt that Damian knew *exactly* how to love her.

"Please, love. Let me." He explored her bare skin, teasing and caressing.

She no longer had the strength to resist. Her body—and her heart—ached for him. "Yes. Go ahead."

Damian kissed her body, running his tongue and lips over

every inch of her skin. He teased her nipples and sucked them, tugging and biting until she arched and moaned, begging for more. He licked her belly, her navel, her hips, and gently parted her legs. Crouching between them, he buried his nose in her triangle of curls and inhaled deeply.

"Your scent is like springtime," he said. "Springtime, after the last snow melts, as the flowers push up through the earth and the leaves bud on the trees. Everything is green. Green and fresh and reborn." He inhaled again. "You smell alive. So alive. I'll never tire of your scent, *mo cridhe*."

"You don't think I'm too..."

"Hmm?" His face was still buried in her curls.

"Hairy." She squeezed her eyes shut. "I'm too hairy down there."

His head popped up. "What?"

Suzanne turned into the pillow. "You heard me."

"Why would you think that?"

"My fiancé. He used to—"

"Never mention him again." Damian did not yell, nor was his voice stern, but its tone left no doubt he meant business.

"I didn't mean to upset you."

"You don't upset me. You upset yourself when you speak of him, and *that* upsets me. He has no place in our bedroom, *mo cridhe*."

"I—"

"Besides, your hair is beautiful. Every part of you is beautiful. The hair on your head is thick and strong and lovely. So of course, you will have an abundance of hair on the rest of your body. Look at me. I'm the same way."

"Yes, but, you're a man."

"So?"

"Damian, you know what I mean."

He tilted his head and gazed into her eyes. "Do you still have feelings for your fiancé?"

"Of course not." Suzanne turned away. "And he's not my fiancé."

"That's how you've referred to him every time you've brought him up."

"Oh." She swallowed. "Old habits are hard to break, I guess. We only ended our relationship a few weeks ago. But no, I don't have feelings for him. Not anymore."

"Then why do you keep mentioning him?"

"I don't know, actually."

"I do. I think you do have feelings for him. I think he hurt you badly. But there's one thing you need to realize."

"What?"

"You're mine now, and I won't tolerate you talking about him." Again, his voice wasn't stern, but he clearly expected to be obeyed. "I won't tolerate you even *thinking* about him. Is that understood?"

"Just who the hell do you think you are?"

Damian didn't answer. Instead, he buried his face between her legs and began to suck her. Relentlessly. No teasing and caressing. He dived right in.

"Oh my God." Suzanne groaned. It was good. So damned good.

Then a knock on the door.

"Shit."

"Tell whoever it is to go away." Damian's voice was muffled as he continued to lick her.

Suzanne said nothing as the knocking continued.

"Suze?"

"It's Isabella," Suzanne said. "My cousin."

"Get rid of her."

"Damian." She tried to move, but he held her down. "Damian!"

"I won't stop. I need you. I need this."

She gasped as his tongue circled her clit. A few seconds more, and—

"Suze, open up. It's me!"

"Damian."

No reply. Her orgasm was imminent. *God, I want to come.* But Isabella wasn't leaving. She took a deep breath and then forcefully scooted backward and broke the suction of Damian's mouth.

"Just a minute, Bell." Suzanne jumped off the bed and began rummaging around for something, anything, to cover her body.

"Damn it!" Damian's bellow vibrated in the still air of the room.

Suzanne turned to him. His green irises swirled around his black pupils.

He left the bed and went into the bathroom, slamming the door. Suzanne heard the rush of the shower.

Quickly, she pulled on some sweats and opened the door, just barely. Isabella appeared well rested and radiant. "Morning, Bell."

"Are you okay? I swear I heard a guy in here."

Suzanne gulped. "A guy?" She shook her head, hoping like hell her cheeks weren't flushing. "Of course not."

Isabella raised her eyebrows and let out a short huff. "If you say so. It's ten. Surely you've gotten enough sleep by now. Let's do something today."

Suzanne cleared her throat. "What did you have in mind?"

"I don't know. How about we go into town? I'm dying to explore."

Suzanne bit her lip. She had no desire to return to the village where she'd nearly been raped. "I don't know."

"Oh, it'll be fun. Get showered and dressed. I'll be back in half an hour."

Suzanne closed the door, frowning, as Damian stepped out of the bathroom wrapped in a towel. His hair was a mass of dripping black waves. She went to him and pushed back a stray curl. Cold. Ice cold. He had taken a cold shower.

"Oh, Damian, I'm sorry."

"What did she want?"

"She's coming back in half an hour. She and I are going into town."

"No."

"You can't keep me here."

"You're not safe out there."

"Come on. It's broad daylight."

He cocked his head, obviously thinking and then put on his jeans, leaving his boxers and shirt on the floor. "Fine. Go. I'll stay here and move my things back into this room."

He couldn't possibly still be on that kick. "Um, about you moving in. Don't you think we should talk about this?"

He opened the bedroom door, his skin still wet and glistening from the shower, the muscles in his bare chest flexed.

"Aren't you going to answer me?"

"No."

6

Suzanne squirmed with unease in the passenger seat as Isabella drove into Padraig. How had the Beetle gotten back to the castle? She'd ask Damian later. No doubt he'd be waiting for her in their room.

Their room.

Suzanne shuddered.

"You're quiet," Isabella said. "Is something wrong?"

"No. Actually, yes." Suzanne cleared her throat. "I went into town last night."

"Oh?"

"Yes, after dark."

"You went into a strange town by yourself after dark?" Isabella shook her head. "That isn't like you, Suze."

Suzanne jerked her head suddenly. It *wasn't* like her. Not at all. What on earth had she been thinking?

"Oh, Goddess," Isabella said.

"What?"

"It was the lunar energy. I should have warned you."

"About what?"

"When you drew in the energy of the Goddess the other night, you drew in her power also. It makes you feel invincible."

"But I didn't feel invincible. I just didn't really think about what I was doing."

"It's not conscious, Suze. The first time I drew down the moon, I went sky diving the next day."

"But you're terrified of heights."

"See what I mean?"

"Lord."

"At least you're all right. We can be thankful—"

"Uh, actually—"

"Dear Goddess, what happened?" Isabella turned her head, looked at Suzanne, and then turned back abruptly to keep her eyes on the road.

"I'm fine. Really. But I did run in to a bit of trouble."

Isabella pulled the Beetle over to the side of the road. "Tell me."

As the words poured from Suzanne's mouth, she found herself weeping. How had she managed to get herself into such a horrible position?

Isabella stroked her arm.

"Thank goodness you weren't hurt. The power of the moon must have helped you get away. It doesn't make you invincible, but it does give you a little boost that you might not otherwise have. But you still need to use common sense."

Suzanne shook her head. "It wasn't the Goddess. It was Dougal's son."

"What?"

"He rescued me. He... From out of nowhere, he came on a Harley."

"Damian?"

"Yes. Have you met him yet?"

"No, but I've talked to Dougal about him. In fact, Dougal talks of nothing but him. He's a doting daddy."

Suzanne said nothing.

"There's still a simple explanation. The energy of the Goddess called to Damian, and he—"

Suzanne shook her head. "He said he smelled me."

"Pardon?"

"He smelled that I was in danger, and he knew exactly where to find me."

"I've never heard of anything like that."

"Neither have I, but truthfully, I didn't much care at the time. I still don't. I'm just thankful he showed up."

"So am I. Goodness." Isabella turned the key in the ignition and started the engine. "I see now why you didn't want to go to town today. We can go back if you want."

Back. It was tempting. But Damian would be there, and Suzanne wasn't up to facing him just yet. "No. I'll be fine. We need to get to know this town anyway since we'll be here for a while."

Isabella nodded "And you need to report what happened last night. Or have you already?"

"No."

"Suze, you know better than that."

She did know better than that. But for now, she wanted to forget it. She didn't respond to Isabella.

"Oh Suze, I'm so sorry I brought you here," Isabella said. "I wanted to get you away from the memories of Wade, but I've only made things worse."

"None of this is your fault, Bell."

"I should have thought to warn you about the power of the moon. Especially here. The energy was *magnified* somehow. I've never sensed anything like it. If anything had happened to you, I'd never have forgiven myself."

"Nothing happened. I'm fine."

"Yes." Isabella didn't seem convinced as she maneuvered the car back onto the road. "At least you got to meet Damian. Tell me what he's like."

Suzanne stared at her cousin. Where to begin?

7

When Damian had finished moving his belongings back into his old room, he found his father in the study they shared. They had, unbeknownst to Merlina, wired a room in the cellar with electricity for the sole purpose of using the Internet.

"Anything new?" Damian grabbed a can of soda out of the small refrigerator plugged into the wall.

"I'm afraid not," Dougal said. "I was just checking the web site and the e-mail account. No one has replied to our posts."

"Damn."

"I'm sorry, lad."

Damian let out his breath and furrowed his brow. "Our posts aren't specific enough, Da."

"We've been through this before. If we get any more specific, we risk attracting every lunatic in the British Isles. And the white coats may come after us as well."

"Aye, well—" Damian paced around the small room. "I need to talk to you."

"What is it?"

"A few things. First of all, last night, I had a run in with a few bloodsuckers in Padraig."

Dougal shook his head. "Did you never listen to Merlina and me? You know better than to mess with those creatures."

"I know, I know."

"What were you thinking?"

"It's a long story. I had to go. I was needed."

"What?"

"I'll explain it all, but first, I need you to check something out on the net. When I was knocking them around—"

"You knocked them around? How many were there?"

"Three."

"*Crivvens*, Damian, you could have been killed!"

"I'm fine. I took them out."

"How were you able to take out three vamps?"

"I had incentive. I'll explain later." He ignored his father's questioning gaze. "Right now, I need you to research something. One of them said something as he scented me, a word I'd never heard before."

"What was it?"

"*Vodlak,* or something. I'm not sure how it's spelled."

"It's probably just some vamp swear word."

"Could be, but I got the feeling he was saying it to me, or about me."

"Still could be a swear word."

"Aye, but check it out, will you?"

"Of course." Dougal began punching letters onto the keyboard. "Now, tell me, what were you doing fighting three vamps?"

Damian sighed. Honesty was important if he and his father were ever to solve the mystery of his existence. "I scented a female I wanted. She was in trouble."

"I see."

"It's nothing I've ever sensed before. I mean, I've desired females before, but this one was different. I had to have her. I had to save her. I actually…"

"What?"

"I scented her for the first time in the tower the other night, during the full moon."

Dougal stopped typing and gazed at his son. "You're not serious?"

"Aye, but it's the only thing I recall."

"It's a start. You've never remembered anything that happens during the change before."

"True."

"Puzzling, though, because there weren't any females—" Dougal cocked his head. "Oh, Merlina's granddaughter?"

"No. Her cousin. Suzanne."

"Ah. Miss Wood."

"She's beautiful."

"Aye, she is. They both are. But lad, you can't possibly—"

"I can't help it." Damian's groin tightened at the mere thought of Suzanne. "She's mine, Da. I don't know how I know it, but she's mine. I'm staying in her room with her."

Dougal stood up and faced his son with fire in his eyes. "You're *what*?"

"I've moved my stuff back into my old room. Her room. I need to be with her."

"Have you gone daft, lad? I won't allow that."

"Sorry, Da. It's already done. She's mine."

"I raised you better than this, Damian. You can't force a woman."

"I'm not forcing her. I just need to be near her."

"*Help ma boab.*" Dougal sat back down facing his monitor. "How does the lass feel about this?"

"She's attracted to me."

"But how does she *feel* about it?"

"She doesn't understand. But the truth is, Da, I don't understand it either. So that's one more thing to research. Why do I desire this woman? I can't get enough of her scent. I want to be near her all the time. I want to protect her. Lie with her. Impregnate her."

"Oh, for God's sake. Is she all right? The vamps didn't hurt her?"

"No. I got there in time."

"Thank God for that."

"Trust me, I have."

"But you don't believe in God."

Damian regarded his father, his jaw clenched. "I do now."

8

Fortunately, when Isabella saw the cute little bookstore, she forgot all about Damian.

"Oh Suze, we've got to go in there." Isabella parked the VW in a dirt alley behind the Lunar Eclipse Bookshop and pulled Suzanne around to the front and into the store.

Suzanne rolled her eyes skyward as she took in the displays of tarot cards, books on witchcraft and moon magick, and incense and herbs. This was paradise for Isabella, pure torture for Suzanne. She found a book of Celtic philosophy and leafed through it, looking up from time to time to see Isabella put another bunch of herbs into the basket she carried.

Bored with the Celts, Suzanne picked up a guide to the Tarot. *I really am desperate.* Out of the corner of her eye, she saw a tall man approach Isabella. Strange that he wore dark glasses inside. The two began a conversation, with Isabella babbling and smiling as was her way. Suzanne put down her book and went to join them.

"Hey, there you are," Isabella said. "I'd like you to meet the owner of this shop."

The black-haired man removed his sunglasses to reveal blue eyes.

Cold eyes.

Icy eyes.

Suzanne's stomach knotted. She grabbed Isabella's arm and struggled for balance.

"You!"

9

"What is it, Suze?" Isabella said. "You're hurting my arm."

"It's... It's..." She pointed at the owner of the Lunar Eclipse.

"This is—" Isabella began.

"Rex," Suzanne said stiffly. "We've met."

"Yes, Rex Donnelly," Isabella said, her eyes wide. "When did you meet?"

"Aye, when indeed?" Rex echoed. "Sure and I'd remember meeting such a lovely lady."

Suzanne swallowed. Her heart pounded against her bosom like a bass drum.

"Surely you recall, Mr. Donnelly. Last evening, you threw me into a den of lions."

"Suzanne," Isabella said. "Perhaps you're mistaken."

"Bull, Bell. This guy handed me over to the three who tried to rape me! We need to call the cops. Are they even called cops here? I'll call Scotland Yard, I will!"

Rex moved away from Suzanne. "I'm so sorry. You've obviously had a traumatic experience. But I assure you, we've never met. Perhaps it was someone who looked like me."

"With your same name?"

"Someone gave you my name. It happens. Criminals rarely use their own name, Miss—"

"Wood," Suzanne snapped. "Suzanne Wood. And I'll be pressing charges."

"Suze—"

"Isabella, we're leaving."

"Look, Miss Wood," Rex said. "I'd hardly have kept my business going here in Padraig for over a decade if I made a habit of aiding and abetting molesters of women."

"I have no idea whether your business would have flourished here. So far, I'm hardly impressed with Padraig. Now, if you'll excuse me—"

"Suze," Isabella said. "Isn't it possible that Mr. Donnelly's telling the truth? It could have been someone else."

Rex cleared his throat. "When did this alleged crime take place?"

"Last night, as you well know, outside Café Oxter."

"Then there's no problem. I was at home last night. My sister will vouch for me. We share a flat."

"Suzanne," Isabella said, "I know how much you're hurting right now. But can you at least accept the possibility that you're mistaken? I mean, Mr. Donnelly here owns a shop devoted completely to white magic and the healing arts."

Suzanne scoffed. "I am so damn sick of you and your magic! It's all a bunch of lunacy and you know it. I'm going to find a cop. Or a Scotland Yard guy. Or whatever the hell you people have around here that passes for law enforcement." She headed for the exit in a huff, Isabella and Rex on her heels.

"Allow me," Rex said. A bell jingled as he opened the door, and the sunlight cast a ray on his forearm.

"Mr. Donnelly—" Isabella began.

"It's Rex," he said. "And don't worry about it. I may be questioned, but nothing will come of it. My sister knows where I was last night, and she's a pillar of Padraig." He reached toward Suzanne.

She seethed. Jagged anger rose from her belly to her throat. "Don't you touch me!"

"I'm sorry," Rex said. "It's just a speck of lint." He brushed her arm lightly, letting his touch linger on her forearm for a moment.

Suzanne inhaled, and her anger dissipated in a glow of pink haze that radiated through her body. Her pulse slowed, and she began to relax. Perhaps she was mistaken after all. He seemed like a perfectly nice man. "Look, Mr. Donnelly—"

"Rex."

"Yes, Rex. I may have overreacted. Maybe I've misjudged you. You don't seem—"

"It's quite all right, Miss Wood. You've clearly been through an ordeal. Would you like me to call a constable for you?"

"No, no. I'm fine, really. I would rather forget it all, to tell you the truth."

"Suze, you know you should report it," Isabella said.

"Yes, yes. And I will." Suzanne inhaled deeply, wondering how she ever could have mistaken this nice shop owner for the accessory to her near rape. "Please accept my apology."

"No apology is necessary," Rex said. "I hope to see you lasses again soon."

"Of course," Isabella said. "This is a wonderful shop. I'm sure I'll be in often for supplies."

Isabella linked arms with Suzanne as they walked back to the car. "Are you ready to report this?"

"Not yet," Suzanne said. "I want to go back to the castle. There's someone I need to see."

"Who?"

Suzanne imagined strong arms holding her, protecting her, helping her forget the evil in Padraig.

"Damian," she said softly.

10

Rex closed the shop, headed downstairs to his basement flat, and stopped in the kitchen for an ice pack to soothe his burning arm. *Damn sun.* His nostrils flared as he pounded on the door to the far bedroom and kicked it in. He roused the sleeping figure on the bed. "Get your ass up, Markus. You have a hell of a lot of explaining to do."

His sister's voice came from the doorway. "What on earth has gotten into you, Rex?"

"Stay out of this, Viveca. Your good-for-nothing son damn near outed us last night!"

Markus sat up, rubbed his eyes, and then yowled in pain.

Viveca ran to his bedside. "Markus, darling! What happened to you?"

Markus cleared his throat and raked his fingers through his tangled blond hair. "Had a bit of a run-in."

"I gift wrapped that American lass for you," Rex said through clenched teeth. "A nice pretty girl, and I handed her to you on a platter, all because I promised my dear sister I'd make sure you fed. Was it too much to ask for you to keep your end of the bargain?"

"Please, Rex, he's hurt." Viveca smoothed her son's hair.

"Poppycock. He'll be healed by nightfall, and you know it." Then, to Markus, "Care to explain why the little lady left with her memories *intact*?"

Markus groaned. "Sorry Unc. We were waylaid a bit."

"So you and those other two moron cronies of yours couldn't handle one woman?"

"Well, she *was* tall."

Rex raised his fist, but Viveca stopped him. "Rex, he's already been beaten."

Rex exhaled sharply "This is no joke, Markus."

"Aye, Uncle, I know. Sorry and all that."

"I swear, Viveca, if he wasn't your son..." Rex paced around the room. "Listen to me. You and the others need to lie low until this blows over. I managed to soften her up with a little mind control, but it's too late to completely erase her memory. It's already gone into long term. If she recognizes you—"

"Hell, I'm no' afraid of that."

"You should be. Our very existence depends on flying under the radar."

"For God's sake, Rex, this is Padraig, not Edinburgh or Glasgow," Viveca said. "Everyone knows we're here."

"Discretion is still important. And from now on, your son is on his own. I'll no longer see to his feedings."

"But you know what happened the last time."

"He'll just have to control himself." He turned to Markus. "Won't you?"

"Aye. I'll control myself. Ouch!" He touched his split lip, which had opened and oozed blood.

"That must have been a strong woman," Viveca said. "Was she one of those American martial artists or something?"

Markus shook his head. "It wasn't her. A bloke came after her. He was..." He shook his head again. "I still can't believe it."

"Believe what, pet?"

"I wouldn't believe it if I hadn't smelled it myself. He was *Voldlak*."

Rex jerked forward. *"What did you say?"*

"You heard me."

Viveca's mouth dropped into an oval. "Not possible. They don't exist. They're a myth."

Markus coughed up blood and spat into his hand. "Evidently not."

Chills ran up Rex's neck as he contemplated his nephew's words.

Voldlak.

Blood wolves.

The vampire brotherhood had chased all the werewolf packs out of Scotland centuries before. Those had been a mutant race who spread their disease through the bite. Violent and angry, they menaced entire cities, turning as many as they could as vengeance for their own fate. Rex's people, as well as humankind, were better off without them.

But *Voldlak*.

Wolf shifters who were born, not made, with a bite so deadly it could kill a human or vampire without even breaking the skin.

The legend had been passed down for millennia, but to Rex's knowledge, no vampire had ever seen one. Or smelled one. So how would Markus know?

His nephew was such a moron. If he wasn't the son of his favorite sister...

"You're mistaken," he said. "It was a foreigner with a strange scent. That's all."

Markus shook his head violently and coughed again. "I swear it wasn't."

"But how would you know?"

"Don't ask me, but I know. Call it intuition."

Rex scoffed. "There are many things I could call it, Markus, but intuition isn't one."

"Rex," Viveca said, "he may speak the truth."

"How could he?"

"You know it's said that the *Voldlak* are mortal enemies of the vampires, and each know the other instinctively by scent."

"This is Markus we're talking about, Viveca. He's not even a full-blooded vamp."

Viveca's green eyes flashed anger. "You promised you'd never mention that!"

Rex exhaled and tried to melt away some of his stress. He wasn't being fair to his sister. "I'm sorry." He turned to Markus. "Tell me more."

"He lives here. I've seen him before, but never noticed his scent until last night."

"You know him, then?"

"Aye." Markus winced as fresh blood trickled from his mouth wound. "'Twas the younger MacGowan. Damian."

11

Suzanne's heart leaped at the thought of seeing Damian. For once, she let the lawyer in her slumber and didn't stop to analyze her feelings. She ran straight up to her room and flung the door open. He lay upon the bed reading and looked amazing in faded jeans and a simple black T-shirt.

"Hello, love." His gaze rose to meet hers.

She ran to him and pounced on the bed.

He chuckled and opened his arms. "Happy to see me?"

"Yes. Yes, yes, yes. I don't know why, but *yes*."

She knelt next to him as he feathered his fingers across her cheek. "Perhaps because you recognize in me what has been missing in your life, as I have, in you."

His mesmerizing jade irises swirled as he gazed into her grey ones. He reached for her hand and kissed it, and then he jolted as he began to nibble on her forearm.

"Where have you been, lass?"

"In town. With Isabella. You knew where I was going."

"Who touched you?"

Suzanne jerked her arm away. "What do you mean? No one touched me."

Damian's eyes swirled and his body tensed against her.

"You're okay, then?"

"I'm fine. I swear."

"I don't want anyone touching you."

"Don't worry."

"No one but me, that is." His eyes softened. "I want to be the one to touch every part of you. Your body. Your heart. Your soul."

She sighed. "You say the loveliest things to me." She took his hand in hers, kissed it, and then touched his fingertips gently. "Your fingers look much better."

"Some of Merlina's special salve. I'm a quick healer."

She smiled. "I'm glad. And your back?"

"Much better, as well."

"Are you ever going to tell me what happened to you?"

"Eventually."

"How about now?"

"How about you kiss me first?"

He pulled her down on top of him until her body covered his. She met his mouth eagerly, kissed him lightly, and ran the tip of her tongue over his fleshy lips. He responded, parting his lips and tasting her, caressing the inside of her cheeks with his silken tongue. Suzanne sighed into his mouth. She had never tasted anything quite like Damian. His flavor was unique and intoxicating, and she couldn't get enough of it. Boldly, she deepened the kiss, thrusting her tongue into his mouth, and then bit his lips and tugged on them.

"Mmm," she said. "You taste so good, Damian."

He pressed his lips to her neck and inhaled. "I was just thinking the same thing about you." He inhaled again and groaned. "And you smell even better."

Suzanne giggled. What was that? Suzanne Wood didn't *giggle*. But there was no other way to describe the girlish laugh that escaped her. "Why do you like my smell so much?"

"Mmm. I don't know. But I can't get enough of it. Of you."

She giggled again. "I don't understand."

"Don't you like my scent?"

"I don't know that you have one."

"I do. Everyone does. Here." He cupped her face and led her to his neck. "Smell me."

"Damian—"

"Come on. Just try it."

"Okay." She buried her face in his neck and inhaled. Cloves again. And musk. Musky man. A little salt. Did salt even have a smell? And wood. Sandalwood or cedarwood. Maybe some patchouli? She was grasping at straws. It was indescribable. It was just...Damian. And it was fantastic. She inhaled again, pressed her lips to the curve of his neck, and kissed him gently. Tiny butterfly kisses. His whispered moans fueled her desire, and she nipped at him, gentle little love bites, and laved him with her tongue. And she made little noises. Almost like a purr. Who was this strange woman?

"You like?" Damian asked huskily.

"I like," she said. "I like a lot."

"See, I have a smell."

"Oh yes, you do." She inhaled again and licked the pulse point on his throat. "You smell wonderful."

"Mmm hmm. See what I mean? You're mine. And I'm yours."

"Oh, Damian."

"It's true, Suzanne. You'll understand soon enough."

"I want to. Really I do. But in the meantime"—she kissed his chiseled jaw line—"shouldn't we get to know each other a little better?"

He smiled against her face. "I've no objection to that."

"Good. Why don't you take me out on a date? Or something."

"I suppose we could. How about tonight?"

"Works for me."

"All right. And in the meantime, we can spend the afternoon making slow, sweet love."

"Um, Damian?"

"Hmm?" He ran his tongue along the outside of her ear and then dipped it inside. She shivered.

"Don't you think we should get to know each other better before we, you know."

"I know all I need to know. You're mine." He nuzzled her neck. "And I want you. Need you. Now."

"Please—"

"*Now, Suzanne.*"

He held her tightly against him and found her mouth with his. Swiftly he moved her under his body and covered her, his arousal apparent against her thigh. She couldn't help returning his kiss, though she struggled beneath him.

Tearing her mouth away, she panted and gasped. "Damian. Please, Damian. Listen to me."

"What?" He lifted his head and looked into her eyes, his now-familiar jade irises swirling with need.

"Just when I start to feel like I want this, you get all domineering and aggressive. Why can't we get to know each other first?"

"I need you," he said adamantly.

"I know." Suzanne tried to make her voice soothing. "I think I need you too. I do need you, although I don't have a clue as to why. But I'm not comfortable sleeping with someone I've known for less than twenty-four hours. Try to understand."

"Please, *mo cridhe*."

Her heart melted as he gazed at her. His wavy hair fell into his eyes. His lips were dark and swollen from their kisses, and she imagined them traveling over every inch of her body. She sighed. Why fight it? She wanted this as much as he did. "Can we still have a date later?"

His beautiful mouth curled into a knowing grin. "Of course, *mo cridhe*. I'd do anything for you. One day, you'll know that."

"I know that now."

"One day, you'll believe it."

"What's the difference?"

"It's the difference"—he brushed his lips over hers and gently sucked at them—"between your mind"—he swirled his tongue into the shallow cove of her ear and softly blew into it—"and your heart."

"Oh." Here she was again, about to climax from words alone. This man affected her in so many ways. She couldn't wait to uncover every one of them. "You win, Damian." She touched his cheek and gently caressed it with her thumb. "Let's make love."

He groaned as he lowered his mouth to hers and kissed her hard, feasting on her. She responded with lustful enthusiasm, their lips and teeth clashing together. She arched her body into his and thrust upward against his erection, imagining it plunging into her.

"Suze?"

Suzanne turned her head and broke the kiss with a soft smack. There stood Isabella, blond and beautiful, framed by the wide open door.

"Suze," she said again. "Uh, is there anything you want to tell me?"

12

Damian's head popped up, and he turned toward Isabella. "God a'mighty, did you think of knocking, lass?"

Suzanne blinked into Damian's blazing eyes. Again, his anger was palpable. She felt it as if it were coming from her own body.

"It's not her fault," she said to the man still lying atop her. "I left the door open."

"Of all the..." He rolled off her, stood, and silently stalked to the bathroom and slammed the door.

Suzanne knew she should feel embarrassed, but she felt nothing more than relief that such a fine specimen as Damian hadn't been mesmerized by Isabella's blond beauty. Her breath came in ragged puffs as she squirmed on the mattress and made sure she was still fully clothed.

"Suzie," Isabella said from the doorway, "I'm so sorry. I had no idea."

"You could have walked away, you know."

Isabella nodded. "I considered it, but this isn't like you."

"I know." Suzanne took a large gulp of air and let it out slowly. "I should have shut the door. I should have...well, I should have been thinking more clearly. I can't believe I was about to...you know."

Isabella walked toward the bed and glanced around the room. "I didn't realize you had met someone."

"I didn't. I mean, I did. That is, he's Damian. Dougal's son. The one who rescued me the other night."

Isabella's lips curved upward. "I know you're grateful for his help, but my Goddess, Suze."

"It's not like that." Suzanne shook her head. "You know me, Bell. I don't fall into bed with men I just met."

"Then why did you?"

Suzanne jerked at the whooshing sound coming from her bathroom. Another cold shower, no doubt. "I can't talk about this now. He'll come back out in a minute and—"

Isabella grabbed her hand. "You're coming with me, hon. We're going into my room, and you'll spill the details." She smiled, mischievous. "Every last one."

Suzanne sighed. How could she spill any details when she didn't understand this thing herself? Still, she rose from the bed and let Isabella lead her down the hall. She didn't want to be in her room when Damian came out of the shower.

She plunked down on Isabella's bed face first. "I don't know what's happening," she said into the comforter.

"I can't understand you when you talk into the mattress." Isabella gently pushed her onto her back.

Suzanne's eyes were scrunched shut, her fists clenched.

"Now talk."

"I'm attracted to him."

Isabella snorted. "Of course you are. Who wouldn't be?

What little I saw was amazing." She took one of Suzanne's hands and massaged it lightly, helping her to relax. "But that's no excuse for nearly sleeping with a stranger."

"That's just it. He doesn't feel like a stranger."

"What on earth do you mean?"

"I don't know." Suzanne buried her head in the covers once more.

Isabella pulled her head around. "Hiding doesn't make it go away."

"I know."

"Did he force you?"

Suzanne gulped and tried to steady her breathing. Damian had been persistent, but no, he hadn't forced her. In fact, she somehow knew he never would. She shook her head, saying nothing.

"Then what exactly happened?"

Suzanne squeezed her eyes shut. If she didn't have to look at her cousin, maybe she could talk about this. Her skin warmed as she opened her mouth.

"After he rescued me, he brought me back here. He refused to leave me. He said he wanted me. I said no. He said he wasn't leaving, but that he wouldn't force me. We slept together, in my bed."

Isabella's eyes widened.

"No, I mean we *slept* together. Snoozed. That's all." She squeezed her eyes harder and the pressure crushed against her pupils. "Naked."

She felt as well as heard Isabella's gasp. "So you haven't—"

"No. Not yet."

"When I came to get you this morning?"

"Yes. He was there."

Isabella caressed Suzanne's forearm gently. "You shouldn't feel bad about this," she said. "You've been through a traumatic experience. It makes perfect sense that you would reach out to someone. Sex is the perfect validation of life, and you were nearly killed."

Yeah, yeah, yeah. Isabella didn't understand. Something else hung in the air, but Suzanne couldn't explain it because she didn't know what it was herself. Better to let Isabella think she had nailed it.

"You're right," she said.

"It's a good thing I interrupted you. You might have made a terrible mistake."

Boy, it hadn't seemed like a mistake, but Isabella was no doubt right. Sleeping with Damian so soon after her break up with Wade couldn't lead to anything good.

She nodded. "Thank you."

"No need to thank me. That's what cousins are for." She leaned down and gave Suzanne a quick hug. "There's no harm in getting to know him better, though. You'll be here for several more weeks. Who knows? Maybe the two of you will hook up."

Suzanne shook her head. "No. You're right. It's too soon after Wade." Then, "Oh shit."

"What?"

"I agreed to go on a date with him tonight."

13

She was gone.

Damian walked around the room in a towel, dripping from his cold shower. Gone. Not a huge surprise.

He toweled his hair, pulled on a clean pair of jeans and a T-shirt, and went to the basement to find Dougal. His father sat at the computer, as usual.

"Anything new?" Damian asked.

Dougal shook his head, his face stern. "Sorry, lad."

"What about the word the vamp used?"

"Nothing from the search engines. Except..."

"Except what?"

"Well, it could be a derivative of *volkodlak*, which is a Russian word for wolf hair or hairy wolf."

Damian stretched his arms and rubbed his temple. His head throbbed. Cold showers did that to him. "Wolf hair. The bloodsucker knew something."

"Maybe, but it's not much to go on. I put up some new posts as discreetly as I could. Maybe..."

Damian sighed. "Yeah, maybe."

"What's troubling you, lad?"

"Other than the fact that I morph into a wolf every full moon, you mean?"

Dougal's mouth twisted into a grin. They had both learned to joke about Damian's condition. "Aye, lad, other than that."

"Suzanne."

"Ah."

"She is reluctant to lie with me."

"*Crivvens*, lad, will you listen to yourself? Of course she is. She just met you!"

"She wants me. I can tell."

"That may be. But she's a woman. *A foreigner.* She might be homesick. She's in a new country, and she just had a traumatic experience in town. She's no doubt grateful to you, Damian, but you mustn't push her."

"I don't want to push her, Da. I really don't." Damian paced back and forth across the small room. "But when I'm with her, the need is so strong. It's like I'll die if I can't have her."

"You're sure you've never experienced anything like this before?"

"Never."

"Not even during the change?"

"Well, that I can't tell you. You know I have no memories of the change, except for scenting Suzanne the other night."

"Aye, but subconsciously. Does what you're feeling seem familiar at all? In the slightest?"

Damian shook his head, sat down in front of the second computer, and flipped the on switch. "Were you ever in love, Da?"

Dougal leaned back in his chair and smiled. "Aye. Once."

"Before you found me?"

"Aye. She died young. Polio."

"I'm sorry."

Dougal shrugged. "It was a long time ago." He cleared his throat. "Why this talk of love, lad? Is that what you're feeling?"

"I don't know. Even I know the absurdity of falling in love with someone I've known only for a day."

"Love's a strange thing. I think I fell in love the first day."

Damian arched his eyebrows. "Indeed?"

"Aye."

Damian turned back to the computer. "How do I get a woman to fall in love with me?"

"*Michty me*, I've no idea, lad. 'Twas a long time ago."

"Come on, Da."

"Well, ease up, for one. Stop pushing her and try wooing her."

"*Wooing* her?"

"Aye. Pick her a bouquet of wild flowers. Take her on a walk around the castle grounds. A picnic on the hills. That sort of thing."

Damian turned to face the computer monitor and typed "how to woo a woman" onto the Google bar. *Och! Over a million hits!*

He clicked on the first. This was going to be a long afternoon.

14

Markus cursed as he rose from his bed to take a leak. He hadn't felt this bad in decades. Damn Damian MacGowan. The bloke was tall and muscular, but Markus should have been able to take him out.

He relieved himself and swallowed six ibuprofen for his throbbing head.

He sniffed. His mother's scent lingered, but she wasn't in the flat. He breathed deeply. He scented Rex above, minding the store. Then the bloodlust hit.

A human entered the shop, and a light truffle-laced scent wafted downward. Androgens. Male, mid thirties, probably blond. His under-scent was peppery and softly floral, not the more herbal aroma of dark hair. The gush of the customer's blood thrummed in Markus's ears. Male blood hadn't touched his tongue in months. He preferred the sweet tang of a female, but a male, laced with musk and testosterone, was a pleasure to be savored, if only once in a while. He had no taste for males sexually, but their blood held a power all its own.

Damn.

He hadn't fed last night, and he needed sustenance. Quickly, he trod to the kitchen and grabbed a sealed bag of sheep's blood out of the refrigerator. He couldn't exist long on animal blood due to his paternity, but it would keep the lust at bay until dark. He ripped the packet open and drank. The acrid thickness of the liquid burned his throat. How did Mum and Rex live on this rotgut?

His hunger sated for the time being, he returned to his bedroom and fired up his computer. Time to do a little research.

Damian MacGowan had bloodied the wrong vampire.

15

Suzanne rose to answer the knock on her bedroom door. Although no one stood outside, a rectangular box on the floor greeted her. She picked it up and read the attached note.

"These confections aren't near as sweet as you, but I hope you enjoy them. I'll come for you at six bells. Damian."

Suzanne's lips curved into a grin. She assumed six bells meant six o'clock. She checked her watch. Four thirty. She had an hour and a half to get ready. But what to wear? She had no idea where they were going or what they would do.

Pants, she decided. Definitely pants. They would probably take Damian's motorcycle, and hiking up a skirt wouldn't be very attractive. She chose a pair of sleek black flared trousers which hugged her hips, a sage green stretch cotton top that accentuated her full breasts—definitely her best feature—and black leather flats. She decided against sandals for the bike. She had begun to apply makeup when someone knocked again.

Again, no one was there, but a bouquet of pink roses laced with baby's breath sat on the floor with another note.

"This flora pales in comparison to your beauty, love. See you soon. D."

Suzanne's heart thumped and her skin tingled. How could such intense emotions course through her so soon after Wade's betrayal?

But she liked it. She liked it very much.

So different from Wade, he was. Dark and sexy to Wade's auburn perfection. Yet Wade paled next to Damian. Yes, he was chiseled and his azure blue eyes shone with the light of thousand torches. But Damian oozed raw sexuality, natural male strength and power coupled with a sweet vulnerability that made her crave his touch. Wade had never been vulnerable. Never would be.

She placed the vase of roses on her dresser and breathed in their fragrance. She loved the smell of roses, floral and exotic. Her favorite flower in her preferred color. How had he known?

Suzanne went into the bathroom and brushed her hair. A few minutes later, she heard another knock on the door. She ran out, hoping to catch Damian in the act. But again, no one stood on the other side.

Suzanne gasped as she looked down. The most adorable stuffed wolf sat there, with a note secured by a red ribbon around his neck. Suzanne loved wolves. They were her favorite animal. She collected wolf prints and figurines. And at age twenty-seven, several stuffed wolves still graced her bed. But she hadn't brought any of them to Scotland.

She clasped the wolf to her chest, buried her nose in its fur, and hugged it to her bosom. Impetuously, she kissed its head and squeezed it tighter.

Then she remembered the note. She tore it open and read:

"I wish I were in your arms instead of this little lad. Counting the moments until we're together, D."

Suzanne laughed aloud. How had he known she would hug the stuffed animal? Was she that transparent? Apparently so.

She returned to the bathroom, humming a Scottish tune under her breath.

Scotsmen.

Delicious.

When her face and hair satisfied her, she checked her watch. Five thirty. A half hour until Damian would call for her. She lay down on her bed and cuddled her new wolf friend, anticipating her evening with this strange, enigmatic man. She still found it hard to believe that he wanted her.

16

Damian's heart raced as he knocked on Suzanne's door. This wooing thing was more difficult than he had imagined. There were so many different ideas, so many varied ways to make a woman fall for a man. After an hour of net surfing, though, a couple of things had stood out. Those few ideas that everyone seemed to agree on.

Send flowers.

Check.

Send candy.

Check.

Send a teddy bear.

He had cheated on that one. He liked the wolf a lot better, and he had somehow felt she would as well.

There were other things he would try later.

A moonlit walk.

A visual caress.

A kiss in the middle of a sentence. He still didn't understand that one, but he was willing to try anything.

But first, dinner.

His breath caught in his throat when she opened the door.

She was beautiful. Everything about her appealed to him. Her silky hair flowing in soft waves down her back, her sparkly gray eyes smiling into his, her lush body covered in sage green and black. *Those breasts, oh God, those breasts.* A more enticing pair didn't exist anywhere on the planet. His skin heated, and he began to stiffen. *Damn, now isn't the time.*

"Hi," she said.

"Hi, love." He curled his lips into a smile that he hoped she found attractive.

"Come on in." She stepped aside for him to enter.

He pulled her close and kissed her chastely on the cheek. It took tremendous effort not to rip her clothes into shreds and carry her to the bed.

"Thank you for the gifts," she said. "I loved them all. Every single one."

"You're welcome, love."

"So—" She cleared her throat. "What are we doing tonight?"

"What would you like to do?"

"Well, I'm hungry. Dinner would be a good start."

"Perfect. We have reservations."

"Where?"

"Not anywhere in Padraig."

"Thank God," Suzanne said. "Where, then?"

"Thurso. It's only forty-five minutes away."

"Am I dressed okay? For the bike, I mean."

"You look perfect." He cupped her cheek and gently rubbed his thumb over her bottom lip. It felt like silk. "And we're not taking the bike. We're taking my car."

"You have a car?"

"Of course. A Bentley."

Suzanne's eyes widened and her mouth formed an oval. A perfectly luscious oval. "A Bentley? Wade couldn't even afford a Bentley. How on earth, Damian?"

He smiled, eager to share with her his good fortune. "I assume Wade is the moron who betrayed you?"

"Yes, and he's loaded. Old money from New England."

"Loaded?" Damian found American English confusing at times.

"Rich. Wealthy. Affluent." She regarded him with an adorable pout. "You know, loaded."

"Aye, I understand." Damian cleared his throat and pulled her into an embrace. "Then it gives me great pleasure to tell you, sweet lass, that I, too, am loaded."

"How?" She pulled away slightly. "What do you do for a living, Damian?"

"I'm a writer."

Her lips formed that adorable oval again. She kissed his cheek, and a fire ignited within him.

"I could write thirty pages on the color of your lips alone. Or your sparkling gray eyes. Or your incredible breasts."

He winked. She blushed. Damian wondered if the color stopped at her neck or kept going. He hoped it kept going. His cock was granite hard in his trousers. How was he going to make it through this evening?

"I want to hear all about your writing. You're obviously very successful, to be able to afford—"

He cut her off with a kiss, nibbling across her upper lip and then the lower, and flicked his tongue in the seam until she parted for him. He kissed her slowly, possessively, tasting every crevice of her mouth. She sighed into him, surrendering, and he deepened his assault and plundered her. He slid his hands down the neckline of her shirt in search of those plump breasts.

She pulled away, catching her breath. "I-I was in the middle of a s-sentence."

"Aye."

"And you kissed me. You cut me off."

"Aye. A kiss in the middle of a sentence. One of the ways to woo a woman."

Suzanne burst into giggles. "What in the world are you talking about?"

"Wooing, love. Don't you want to be wooed?"

"Uh, sure, I guess." She smiled at him. "Exactly what is going on here?"

"My Da said I should stop pushing you and start wooing you."

Suzanne cupped his cheeks and smiled into his eyes, the golden flecks in her irises dancing. "You are the sweetest man on the planet, Damian MacGowan." She giggled again. "Just angelic."

"Ah, so the wooing is working, then?"

She kissed his lips, brushing her mouth softly over his. "It's working so well, in fact, that if you keep it up, we'll never get to dinner."

"Well, then." He pulled her into his arms and lowered his head.

"But—" She pushed him away. "You promised me a date. And I'm starving. So let's go, okay? I can't wait to see Thurso."

17

Isabella dusted off the two books she found in the bottom drawer of her grandmother's bureau.
Book of Shadows.
Merlina was a witch?
Suzanne might be on a date with the gorgeous Damian MacGowan, but Isabella's body hummed with excitement over her find. With hope in her heart and a smile on her face, she opened the first leather-bound volume.

18

"I don't have to eat haggis, do I?"

Damian erupted in laughter, and Suzanne savored the joyful sound. Had she never heard him laugh before? No, she hadn't. She smiled, despite the nausea that thoughts of sheep stomach and innards caused. The restaurant was small and homey, and delicious aromas of garlic and spice wafted around the dining room.

"Not too excited by the prospect, eh, love?"

"Can't say that I am."

"Don't tell my Da, but I don't much like the stuff either. I was thinking more along the line of seafood. We're right on the coast, and it's all fresh and delicious. Do you like seafood?"

"Mmm. I love it." Suzanne closed her eyes. "Except for calamari. It's too rubbery."

"I'm not talking about calamari."

"Fish and chips, then?

Damian laughed again. What a nice sound! "This isn't a

London pub, love. I'm talking about fresh seafood. Mussels and scallops. Or salmon. Scotland has wonderful salmon."

"I love salmon. It's my favorite fish."

"Salmon it is, then." He took her hand. "Do you mind if I order for you?"

"Is that another way to woo a woman?" What fun it was to banter! His demeanor had been so serious before.

He shook his head, and his beautiful mouth curved into a grin. "No, Suzanne. I just thought I might show you some of my favorites. Tell me, is there anything you absolutely won't eat?"

"I have a pretty sophisticated palate, actually, but there are a few things. Goat cheese, for example. I can't stand the stuff."

"Aye. What else?"

"Um, let's see. Not crazy about beets, but other than that, I like most veggies. And lamb. Too gamey for me. But I like all other meats."

"All right. I've a good idea of what to order, then." He gestured to the server. "We'll have the cream of cauliflower soup with caramelized onions, organic salmon with crushed potatoes, green beans, and Arran mustard sauce, and berry trifle for dessert." He turned to Suzanne. "Is a light red wine good for you? Or do you prefer white with fish?"

"Light red would be great with salmon."

"Good." He turned back to the waiter. "A Beaujolais-Villages, I think. Louis Jadot."

"Very good, sir."

"Now, my beautiful Suzanne. You know much about me. What I do. Where I live. What I drive. How I order food."

Suzanne giggled. "You want to know about me?"

"Aye."

"I'm an attorney."

"Pardon?"

"A lawyer. You know, a solicitor."

"Ah. How long have you been a lawyer?"

"Two years."

"And that makes you how old?"

Her cheeks warmed. "Twenty-seven. Kind of an old maid, aren't I?"

His eyes crinkled. "Not at all. I'm thirty-five myself."

"Have you ever been married?"

He shook his head. "Never met the right woman."

"Oh." She couldn't think of anything to say to that, so she changed the subject. "Tell me about your writing. I mean, you must be successful, to drive a Bentley."

"I've had moderate success."

"Has your work reached the States? Would I have read anything you've written?"

His dark eyes glimmered. *God, he's handsome.*

"Perhaps. Have you heard of *The Code of the Wolf*?"

Suzanne's heart thumped. "The international best seller?"

"That's the one." His eyes gleamed at her.

"*You're* David Branson?"

"In the flesh."

"*Oh. My. God.* That's one of my favorite books of all time!"

"I'm glad you enjoyed it."

"Enjoyed it? I *devoured* it. Every producer in Hollywood is trying to buy those rights. Why haven't you sold them?"

"I don't want a movie made from my work. A movie tends to bastardize the original."

"But the money, Damian."

"Do I look like I need any more money?"

Suzanne laughed. "I suppose not. Wow. Amazing."

He smiled at her.

"Why a pen name? You're known as a recluse, you know."

"I *am* a recluse. As for the name, I didn't want anyone to find me. And I'm trusting you with my secret."

"I'll never tell anyone, not even Isabella. But why? You've written a masterpiece. Why don't you want people to know?"

"I have my reasons."

"Will you tell me?"

"Eventually."

"Moderate success, you said. Moderate success." Suzanne glanced down at the bowl of steaming soup the waiter set before her. She inhaled the aroma. "Mmmm, smells good." She took a spoonful, blew on it, and tasted it. Warm and creamy. "Oh, that's wonderful." She chuckled. "Moderate success indeed."

Damian smiled at her, and his green irises swirled in that unique way she had become accustomed to. One eye fluttered for a moment. Then the other.

"Are you all right?" she asked.

"Aye. Why do you ask?"

"It looks like you have something in your eye."

He shook his head. "That was a visual caress. Didn't you like it?"

"A visual caress?" Suzanne shook her head and laughed. "Don't tell me. Wooing, right?"

"Aye. You know me too well."

"You don't have to try so hard."

"You told me the wooing was working, love."

"*You* are what is working, Damian."

What a strange man.

Oh, but what a *man*.

So much for her pact to stay away from him. So much for her rationale that getting involved with anyone this soon after Wade couldn't lead to anything good.

She sincerely hoped they wouldn't be interrupted later.

19

Markus left the flat after sundown. He moved with stealth, sneaking past his mother and Rex. They were so used to his scent that he knew he could get by undetected as long as he was quiet.

Very quiet.

Vampire hearing was quite powerful. Almost as powerful as a vampire's sense of smell.

Although darkness hadn't completely veiled Padraig yet, his hunger forced his exit. The bloodlust needed sating, and he had a taste for a male tonight. He'd thought of nothing else since he had scented the blond male earlier in Rex's shop. His stomach growled and his mouth watered as he walked to the Pit.

Standing by the entrance, he spied Gwennie hustling inside, pouring steaming bowlfuls of cock-a-leekie and cups of tea. As he grasped the door handle, another hand touched his.

"I'm sorry. Pardon me."

American. Auburn hair, nice face, lots of muscle. Markus inhaled. Potent, too. Very potent.

"Not a problem, friend. You're new here?"

"Yeah. Just got in today."

"Sure and there's better places to eat in Padraig than the Pit."

"The Pit?"

"Café Oxter." Markus smiled, careful not to let his fangs show. "Oxter is a Scots word for armpit."

"Oh." The man flushed.

Markus twitched at the hiss of his blood rushing to the surface of his skin. He needed a taste, and he needed it now.

"Aye. I'd be happy to show you a better place, lad. We can get a pint or two while we wait."

The man nodded and smiled. "I heard you Scots were friendly sorts."

"Aye." Markus touched the sleeve of the man's sports coat and shuddered at the rush he felt even through the fabric. "Friendly we are, at that. Come with me."

20

"This is where Isabella and I danced naked the first night we were here."

Damian's eyes widened and his mouth dropped open. The two had returned from Thurso and had taken a moonlit walk around the castle property, ending in the courtyard. Suzanne laughed, throwing her head back, and then she gently pushed his chin upward and closed his mouth. "Watch out for mosquitoes."

Damian said nothing.

"You've been so quiet since we got back," Suzanne said. "I thought for sure that comment would get you."

"We don't call them that here."

"What?"

"Mosquitoes. We call them midgies."

"Oh." Her first comment had gone right over his head, obviously.

"And they love foreigners, by the way. We should get you some bug repellent."

"I'll be fine."

"I'm immune myself. Never been bitten."

"Damian, I don't give a damn about the mosquitoes, or midgies, or whatever. I just told you that Isabella and I danced naked out here. Don't you have anything to say to that?"

"Why?"

"Why did we dance naked?"

"Aye."

"It was Isabella's idea. She needed to draw down the moon or something. It's a ritual she does during the full moon."

"Oh?" Damian looked away. What was bothering him?

"Yeah. She's a witch."

"Mmm hmm." He stared intently toward the sky, the reflective light from the gibbous moon illuminating his beautiful features.

"I just told you my cousin is a witch."

"Aye. I heard you."

"So aren't you going to tell me I'm crazy? That there's no such thing as witches?"

He tore his gaze from the moon and looked into her eyes. "Why would I do that?"

"Well, because—" She let out a huff of air. "Because there's no such thing as witches, that's why."

"Of course there are witches, love. Merlina was a witch. It makes perfect sense for Isabella to be one."

"Merlina was a witch?"

"Aye."

"Oh, God."

"What?"

"Never mind." She changed the subject. Quickly. "You were a million miles away a minute ago. What's wrong?"

"Nothing. I just don't like thinking about the full moon."

"Even if I'm dancing naked under it?" She grinned, teasing. At least she hoped it was a teasing grin. She had no idea. She had never been much of a flirt.

"*Especially* if you're dancing naked under it." He pulled her into a tight embrace and pressed his lips to the soft skin under her ear. "I only want you dancing naked for me."

Suzanne shuddered, and her blood raced through her veins. She lifted her lips for his kiss and melted into the heat of his embrace as he nibbled at her mouth. No one kissed like Damian. He savored her mouth, made love to it. Made her feel like this kiss was the only kiss they would both ever experience. Her flesh quivered and her womb ached, and he hadn't even touched his tongue to hers yet.

Anxious to move things along, she parted her lips and tasted him, outlining his full lips with her tongue. Mmm. Raspberries. The Frangelico they had enjoyed with their dessert. Plus Damian's own musky maleness. Had there ever been a more enticing flavor?

He groaned as he returned her kiss. His beautiful long-fingered hand framed her face and stroked her cheeks. Then he moved one hand to her nape and tilted her head, giving him access to her neck and throat. His talented lips roamed over cheeks and licked her ear, her neck, nibbling, biting, licking to soothe the skin.

"Oh, Damian." Suzanne's voice was soft and husky and sounded as though it came from somewhere else.

"Aye, love."

He continued his assault with his lips while he moved his hands from her neck to her shoulders and then trailed down her arms in feathery caresses. Up her waist he went, settling on her breasts. She tingled all over as he cupped her, rubbing her nipples through her shirt and bra. Her pussy clenched with a need to be filled.

"Ah," she moaned.

Damian lowered his head and bit her nipple through two layers of clothing, but it felt as if she were naked. She pulled his hips to her and ground her pelvis into his erection. She smiled at his groan.

"Aye, love. That's it."

She wanted this man. She wanted to share her body with him tonight in a timeless dance different from anything she had experienced.

"Damian?"

"Hmm?" He bit her nipple again, and she shuddered, her flesh quivering as she nearly lost her balance.

"Let's... That is, I want..." Her voice trailed off as his warm hands slid under her shirt, up her back, and then under the clasp of her bra.

"What, love?" His voice was breathy, raspy. "What do you want?"

"You. I want you."

He scooped her into his arms as if she weighed no more than a child and headed toward the castle. Neither said a word as he ascended the staircase and opened the door to her room.

He laid her gently on the bed and covered her body with his, pushing against her with his cock and kissing her mouth with abandon. She felt every ounce of his passion, his desire for her. Arching her body into his, she moaned his name.

And the unexpected happened.

He broke the kiss and stood up. The fire in his eyes smoldered, but he backed away.

"Damian?"

"I'll go now, love."

"Wh-What?"

"I won't push you."

"It's okay. Push me. For God's sake, push me!"

"Not tonight, *mo cridhe*."

Suzanne's unsated lust burned. He wasn't really going to leave her, was he? After he had been begging her for the last two days?

"If you leave now, Damian, so help me..."

He backed toward the door. "Sweet Suzanne." His sexy Scottish lilt, more pronounced when he was angry or turned on, washed over her like a lusty red wine. "Dream of me."

He backed out the door and shut it.

Well, damn.

21

Now where the hell was he going to sleep? Damian wandered the halls of the castle. All of his stuff was in Suzanne's room.

What had he been thinking?

She wanted him, and he had walked away.

His hunger roused the wolf. His body trembled, but he would not sate himself. Not with anyone but Suzanne. He couldn't bear the thought.

This wooing thing was going to kill him.

Don't fall right into bed with her. Show her she's worth the wait.

Number thirty-two in the first article. Number ten in next. Stupid thing had appeared in nearly all his research.

Of course, the idiots who wrote these—probably all women—didn't say what to do when his urges overpowered him.

He glanced at his watch. Half past one in the morning. He had left Suzanne an hour ago. Had he been pacing all this time?

"To hell with wooing," he said aloud and then ran to Suzanne's room.

He opened the door without knocking. There she was, sprawled on the bed, naked, her brown tresses fanned like gossamer wings against her pillow. Her plump breasts rolled gently with each sweet breath she took. Her legs, slightly bent, tangled in the cotton sheet. Damian took a sharp breath, her loveliness nearly too much to bear. Then he noticed the black curls between her legs. Still moist.

God she was beautiful. Like nothing he had ever seen before. His cock ached for her.

He disrobed quickly and climbed into bed next to her.

"Damian?" Her voice was raw, as though she had been crying.

"Aye. It's me."

She turned to him, wrapped her arms around him, and drew him close.

"Damn it, if you ever leave me like that again, I'll rip your head off."

He chuckled softly. "My mistake, love. All this wooing nonsense. Never again. I promise."

"Do you want to...?"

"In the morning, *mo cridhe*." He feathered a few kisses across her forehead. "Go back to sleep now."

Oh, he wanted to have her. It was a fierce need, a driving hunger. His body yelled from within to climb on top of her and thrust into her, take her, make her his. But a stronger desire overpowered his basal instinct. A need to hold her, protect her, be with her. What he felt in her arms was like nothing he had known before. Security. Safety. True love.

True love? Where had those words come from?

He smiled to himself and inhaled the sweet vanilla fragrance of her hair. Was it possible, after only a few days?

He had known from the first instant that she was his. He didn't understand it, but that didn't make it any less real.

Aye.

True love.

22

Suzanne awoke entangled in Damian's arms. She ran her fingers lightly over his back. The scratches had healed.

Wow.

They had healed fast, hadn't they?

She traced his wolf tattoo. An incredible work of art. But why? Why would he tattoo his entire back? She eyed him up and down. He didn't appear to have any other tattoos. She smiled to herself. She had always wanted a tattoo but had never possessed the courage to get one. Wade would have freaked out. Maybe she would ask Damian to take her to get a tattoo while she was here. It would be a fun souvenir of her few weeks in Scotland.

Few weeks? The words hit her like a bolt of lightning. She didn't live here. She wouldn't be staying. This thing with Damian—it would end.

Sadness hit Suzanne like a harsh rainstorm. She didn't want to leave. She wanted to know Damian better. He was the best thing to come into her life in a long time. But she had a job.

A home.

A life back in the States.

"Oh, Damian." She sighed.

He turned over, opened his eyes, and smiled. "Morning."

"Good morning," she said.

"Sleep well, love?"

"Yeah. You?"

"Aye."

"I'm sorry about last night, Damian."

"You're sorry? About what?"

"I...whatever I did to anger you. To drive you away."

He chuckled softly. "You did nothing, *mo cridhe*. It was me. All me. I was trying to woo you."

"By leaving me hanging?"

"Aye."

"Who in the world told you to do that?"

He shrugged his shoulders. "I'm not sure, but all the articles I read said that I shouldn't push you into bed. And I know I've been...persistent up until now."

Suzanne smiled and raked her eyes over his incredible body. "You have been. But Damian, last night I wanted you. I thought you knew."

"Aye, I knew."

"Then why did you leave?"

"I thought it was what I had to do. To woo you, that is."

"Okay, listen to me."

"What is it?"

"Throw out all that research."

"You mean you didn't like the flowers, the dinner, the moonlit walk?"

"No, no. All that stuff was great."

"I didn't want you to think I did all that just to get you into bed."

"I didn't think that. I wanted to make love with you last night, Damian. I wanted to be close to you. I felt like we connected at dinner. We got to know each other better. When you left, I thought…"

"What, love?"

"I thought you didn't want me anymore. That once you got to know me, you changed your mind."

"Never, love." He sat up and faced her, his swirling eyes boring into hers. "I'll never change my mind about you." He brushed his lips lightly against hers. "Is that why you were crying?"

She nodded and tore her gaze from his. He tipped her chin with his hand and forced her to look into his eyes. "I promise you, Suzanne Wood, I will never change my mind about you." He brushed his lips over hers. "*Mo cridhe*, I love you."

Suzanne gasped as her heart nearly leaped from her chest. "I'm sorry?"

"I said I love you, Suzanne."

"But how?"

"Crazy, I know. Damned if I understand it. But from the first moment I saw you, smelled you, touched you, I knew. You're mine. Always."

Suzanne squirmed, wanting to break away, yet wanting to clamp herself to him and never let go. The overwhelming contradictions gnawed at her gut. "Oh, Damian, I don't know what to say."

"You don't have to say anything."

"But I do. I'm only here for a few weeks. I have a job, a home, a life."

"So you'll start a new life. Here. With me."

"It's not that simple." She breathed deeply. "You know I just got out of a messy relationship. I don't want you to be my rebound guy. That wouldn't be fair to you."

"Rebound guy?"

"You know. The man who picks up the pieces and then moves on."

"I'll never move on."

She covered her face with her hands. What had she gotten herself into? And why was she half ready to drop her entire life and stay in Scotland with a man she had met less than seventy-two hours ago?

Damian gently pulled her hands from her face and replaced them with his own. "I love you. There's not a doubt in my mind. You'll love me someday. I'm sure of it. I want to make love to you now." He pressed his lips to hers. "Now. *Right now*." His brown-green eyes swirled.

Suzanne's breath caught in her throat. "Damian—"

"Now. I've waited long enough for you. I need you. Desperately."

"But I—"

"You were ready to love me last night. I should have taken you then."

Suzanne nodded. "Yeah. You should have. I wouldn't have turned you down."

"And now?"

She lowered her hand to her pillow and found the soft fur of her stuffed wolf. Perfect. A change of subject. "How did you know I love wolves?"

He still cupped her cheeks, and his eyes swirled into hers. "I didn't."

"I collect them. Photos, figurines, stuffed animals."

A lazy half smile curled over Damian's sensuous mouth. "I didn't know, love."

"You have good instincts then, I guess."

"Aye. So I have."

"Do you like wolves?"

He drew his gaze away from hers, still cupping her cheeks. "I wrote about them in my book."

"So you like them?"

He sighed, his eyes a swirly mass of brown and green. And sadness? "I love many things about them. Their strength. Their beauty. Their wildness." He returned his gaze to hers. "Now, *mo cridhe*, will you let me love you as I desire?"

Suzanne's skin tingled with anticipation. Her blood boiled like hot nectar in her veins, the warmth flowing downward to her sexual core. She slowly nodded her head.

He groaned and lowered his mouth to hers. His kiss was deep and passionate. No mouth foreplay this time. He delved in with his tongue and tasted her thoroughly, completely.

Damian's tongue danced around hers, licking, stroking, plunging in and out, mimicking the sex act. Suzanne's pulse raced as she laced her fingers through his waves and pulled him closer, kissing him deeper. If it were possible for two people to mate through a kiss, they were doing it.

Then hands. Hands everywhere. His on her breasts. Hers on his shoulders, caressing his tight sinewy muscle. His cupping her mound, sliding through her slick folds. Hers grasping his cock, stroking it as his shudder rocked through her own body. Heat. Intense heat.

"So wet," he said as he fondled her pussy. "So wet. For me."

She gasped as he slid a finger inside her.

"For you," she echoed, sliding her lips over his neck, his shoulder, down onto his chest, where she flicked her tongue over a brown nipple.

"Aye, love," he said. "Touch me. I'm yours. All yours."

Suzanne's fingers shook as she scraped the golden skin of his chest and licked downward, twirling her tongue through the masculine hair, down to his navel, and then...

She wanted him in her mouth. That beautiful perfectly formed cock. It called to her. *Lick me. Taste me.*

"Aye." He read her mind. "Taste me, love. I ache for it."

Her lips trembled as she opened her mouth to take him. Her tongue touched his tip and he jerked. "God a'mighty, lass, you're killing me."

She smiled, swirled her tongue around him, and reveled in the salty pre-come that emerged. She kissed and nibbled and then prepared herself to take all of him.

Someone pounded on her door.

"Aw, fuck!" Damian jerked away from Suzanne's mouth. "If that's your cousin again, I can't be held responsible for my actions."

Suzanne looked at her lover, crazed with passion and desire, and then she looked down at her own body, flushed with a fiery redness, her pussy swollen and wet.

Damn it, Isabella, why now?

"Just ignore it," she said.

But the pounding continued. "Suze, it's me. I have to talk to you. Please, I've been up all night. It's extremely important!"

Damian stood up and headed toward the bathroom. "Go ahead and see to her. She won't go away. We both know that."

Suzanne ran up behind him, clasped her arms around his waist, and pressed her pebbled nipples into his muscled back. "I'm so sorry."

"Me too." He placed his hands over hers and broke her grasp. He turned and took her into his embrace. "We don't have the best timing, do we, *mo cridhe*?"

She laughed, exhilarated that he wasn't angry. "No. We're going to have to get better at this."

"Aye." He brushed his lips across her cheek. "I love you," he said, "and I *will* make love to you. I need to."

She nodded. "I know. I need it too. Later, okay?"

"Later." He broke the embrace, walked into the bathroom, and shut the door.

The shower whooshed.

Again.

Suzanne pulled on a pair of sweats and a tank top. "What is it?" she demanded, opening the door.

Her cousin didn't apologize or offer any explanation for her behavior, which puzzled Suzanne.

"Get dressed," Isabella said. "We need to talk."

23

"It's a Book of Shadows," Isabella said in response to Suzanne's query about the heavy volume her cousin had plunked into her lap.

The two women sat in Isabella's bedroom, a plate of sweet cakes and a carafe of wine between them. Cakes and ale, Isabella had said, from a recipe of Merlina's. She had labored over them in the powerless kitchen of the castle and then promptly called an electrician in Thurso once dawn had broken. He was due later today to give an estimate and begin work.

"What's a Book of Shadows?"

"It a witch's handbook, of sorts," Isabella said. "Each witch creates her own book, adding to it the spells she writes, her own special potions and tinctures, recipes, and anything else that's important to her craft."

"So your grandmother was a witch, then?"

"So it would appear."

Suzanne sighed and faced her cousin. "So. You interrupted me this morning to tell me your grandmother was a witch? Jesus, Bell."

"No, no, no. I would never do that." Isabella stood, paced around the room in a semi-circle, and then sat back down. "But why would you care if I had interrupted you? Don't tell me you changed your mind about Damian. *Again.*"

"So what if I did?"

"Oh, Suze."

"Look. I know it's a mistake. But it's mine to make. I'll only be here for a few weeks. Why not have some fun?"

"Because that's not you, Suzanne. You don't have fun."

"Hey!"

"You know what I mean. You've never been able to separate sex and love. What makes you think you can start now?"

"I don't know." She smiled. "Maybe you could hex me or something."

Isabella laughed and shook her head. "Oh no, you don't. Magic doesn't exist solely when it serves your purpose. You either embrace it in your life or you don't. You can't have it both ways."

"Maybe I'll embrace it, then."

"Nothing would make me happier, cuz, but I still won't hex you. That's black magic."

Suzanne let out a sharp breath. "Whatever. Let's get back to why you roused me out of an insanely gorgeous man's bed this morning."

"Okay." Isabella sat down on the floor next to Suzanne and opened the second large volume. "The book you're holding has all of Merlina's spells and incantations, her recipes, etcetera. But this one..."

"Yeah?"

"This one was a complete surprise."

"How so?"

"Well, there's a detailed family tree in it, but you'd have no interest in that. There's also a history of Padraig. Apparently—" Isabella cleared her throat. "We're living in spook central."

"Spook central?" Suzanne swallowed her mouthful of cake.

"It's hard to fathom, even for a believer like me, so I know how fantastic this is going to sound to you. Apparently the little town of Padraig is a hangout for entities who are"—she cleared her throat again—"other than human."

"Excuse me?"

"Vampires, for the most part, some ghosts, an occasional demon."

"Oh come on, Bell."

"I know, it's crazy. But Merlina has a whole history in here." She flipped pages of the book in Suzanne's lap. "Evidently, the vampires aren't a bad sort, in general. They're just a different race. An ancient one."

"So should we be wearing garlic around our necks?" Suzanne laughed.

"This is serious, Suze. And no, garlic won't do any good. That's a myth."

"Bell, this whole darn thing is a myth. Your grandmother was obviously off her rocker. Is there Alzheimer's in your family?"

"Not that I know of. Then again, I know next to nothing about the O'Days." Isabella shook her head. "My grandmother wasn't crazy. Dougal would have mentioned it if she were."

"Would he? Maybe he didn't know."

"He's lived here for years."

"That's another thing. Why would Dougal and Damian live here? After all—" Suzanne quickly closed her mouth. She had promised Damian she wouldn't tell anyone he was David Branson. But the question haunted her. Why would he and his father continue to live in a drafty old castle with no electricity, when they could afford to live wherever they wanted?

"I don't know why they live here. Maybe Dougal felt a responsibility to stay with Merlina."

"Don't you think we should ask *them* about Merlina? About whether she had all her, you know, faculties?"

Isabella nodded.

Talk of Damian and Dougal sparked a memory. "Damian knows Merlina was a witch. He told me last night."

"Did he? How did it come up?"

Suzanne giggled. "I told him about our naked dance under the full moon and that you were a witch."

"Oh."

"But Bell, there's a big difference between believing you're a witch—"

"We don't believe, we know," Isabella said adamantly.

"Yeah, yeah, whatever." Suzanne rolled her eyes. "Knowing you're a witch and believing in vampires are two completely different things."

"I won't argue with you there."

"Tell me more of this fairy tale, then. What else did you find about these alleged vampires?"

"Now you're talking like a lawyer."

"I *am* a lawyer."

"Right." Isabella smiled. "They live longer than humans. Their normal life span is about five hundred years. And although the sun won't necessarily kill them, they are extremely sensitive to it. They can't go out in daylight without sunscreen, and even then, they will probably burn within half an hour. Most of them avoid going out during the day."

"Which explains the nightlife in Padraig."

"What do you mean?"

"The other night, when I went out. It was lit up like Vegas."

"Hmmm. Are you beginning to believe, my skeptical cousin?"

Suzanne caught herself. Was she beginning to believe? "No, that's not it."

"Anyway, they need blood to survive. But most of them either drink from each other or subsist on animal blood. The sheep farms around here supply a lot of blood to the vampire population."

"Oh God." Suzanne clutched her stomach. Just the thought of it... She closed her eyes, hugging herself. Her arms suddenly felt chilled, and she rubbed the goosebumps in an attempt to warm herself with the friction. Her heartbeat quickened, and a vision appeared in her mind, of Rex Donnelly leading her behind Café Oxter and pushing her into the arms of a large blond man. Rex's low voice telling the men not to take too much, that he'd bring more later. Six hands poking her, groping her, and then, on her neck—the scraping, the sharpness.

Teeth.

Fangs.

Damn.

They might have raped her, but sexual gratification hadn't been their primary goal. They had wanted her blood.

She had been attacked by vampires.

24

"They have incredible strength, as well," Isabella said. "The weakest vampire is as strong as the strongest human."

"I'm sorry." Suzanne jerked her head back toward her cousin. "What did you say?"

"They're strong. Stronger than humans."

"I see." The fog of that perilous night cleared slowly, and images unfolded on a screen in her mind's eye. The three men—were they indeed men?—attacking her, her heart pounding, her fear a palpable mass of emotion. Their eyes full of hunger, their mouths salivating, their bodies crushed against hers.

Then, out of nowhere, Damian.

He had plowed them into the ground. All three of them. Three vampires with super-human strength, and Damian had pummeled them as if they were the dust beneath his feet. How?

Suzanne shuddered as she erased the images from her

mind. They hadn't been vampires. That was the only logical explanation. Damian couldn't have beaten three vampires.

Of course they hadn't been vampires. What had she been thinking? Vampires didn't exist.

She inhaled, tried to relax and force the chills from her neck. "When does the electrician get here?"

"That was an abrupt change of subject," Isabella said.

"I'm afraid I'm done with this nonsense, Bell. You'll never get me to believe there are vampires in Padraig."

Isabella sighed, closed the book on Suzanne's lap, and placed it on top of her dresser. "To tell you the truth, Suze, I'm not so sure I believe it, either."

"Now you're talking sense," Suzanne said. "What should we do today?"

"I need to stick around. I want to be here when the electrician comes."

"Can't Dougal take care of that?"

"It's my castle now, so it's my responsibility. Plus, I'm the one who's going to be paying for it. I hope the cost won't be too dire."

"You've got Merlina's inheritance."

"Yeah, but that's not much, only fifty grand. It needs to last. Especially if I'm going to stay here."

Suzanne's head nearly spun off her neck. "You're going to what?"

"I've decided to stay here and live at the castle."

"Bell..."

"I'm not like you, Suze. I don't have a big job that pays tons of money waiting for me back home. I'm a part-time waitress who does Tarot readings on the side. I can do that anywhere."

"You'd turn your back on your home? Your country?"

"I'm not turning my back on anything. I'm facing my future. I belong here. I felt it as soon as our plane touched the ground. This is my destiny."

Suzanne's skin iced over. The thought of not having Isabella nearby speared into her heart like a hunting blade. "How can you be sure? We haven't even been here a week."

"I'm sure. There's incredible lunar energy here. I felt it that first night. And so did you."

Suzanne shook her head.

"Don't try to deny it, cuz. I know you felt it. And now that I found Merlina's Book of Shadows, it all clicked together. This is where I belong. I can learn so much here about my family and my craft." She sighed. "About myself."

Suzanne embraced her cousin. "I'll miss you so much, Bell."

"You could stay, you know. Maybe a certain handsome Scotsman might convince you?" Isabella's lips curved into a mischievous grin.

Suzanne sighed. Damian had already all but demanded she never leave. But as irresistibly drawn to him as she was, there remained a mystery, an enigma, surrounding him that she couldn't ignore. Until she knew him better, she wouldn't consider staying, no matter what her heart and body wanted.

"I have a job, Bell. They're expecting me back. They're depending on me."

"I was pretty sure you'd say that." Isabella grinned impishly. "But we'll talk again after you and Damian do the deed."

Suzanne's skin warmed. She rose and strode toward the bed, picked up a pillow, and hurled it at her cousin. "We'd have done it three times by now but for your interruptions!"

Isabella ducked the assault. "*Touché*, cuz. *Touché*."

25

Damian paced the cellar room as Dougal tapped away at his keyboard. *Damn.* He had been so close. So close to finally joining his body with Suzanne's.

"What's troubling you now, lad?"

"She likes wolves, Da. She collects them."

"She, meaning Suzanne?"

"Aye."

"I'm thinking you don't mean she collects real wolves."

"No. Figurines. Prints. Stuffed wolves."

"And?"

"It's got to mean something, doesn't it? This need I feel for her, this knowledge that she's mine?"

"I don't know, lad, but I'll research it. How was your date?"

"Perfect, actually." Damian sat down, his hair still damp from his most recent cold shower. "Until her cousin interrupted us this morning. Again."

Dougal chuckled, his back quivering. "Patience, lad."

"And she talks about going home. I can't bear the thought of her leaving, Da."

"She's only here for a few weeks. Isabella said four, I think."

"Well, then, I've a little over three more to convince her to stay with me."

"I hate to bring up the obvious, lad, but what exactly are you going to tell her about your condition?"

Damian inhaled sharply, paced to the end of the room and back, and then grabbed a Guinness out of the refrigerator. "I've been thinking. I don't think she really needs to know."

Dougal's eyes widened as he stood up. "*Michty me!* Of course she needs to know!"

"No, Da. I'll lose her for sure then."

"How do you know that? Maybe she'll understand."

Damian took a long drink of the dark beer. "Who in the name of God himself could ever understand what I am? I don't even understand it myself. She can't know, Da. She can't."

"Lad—"

"I've thought about it. You can continue to lock me in the tower during the change. I'll tell her I'm out of town on business or something. I already told her who I am and what I do for a living. She'll understand that I need to meet with editors and agents and such."

"And she's too stupid to figure out that you're gone during every full moon?"

"It will work," Damian said. "It has to."

Dougal shook his head. "There's nothing I want more than your happiness. I'd give my life for it. But this'll never work. You've got to be honest with her. How do you expect to build a relationship with this lass if you cannot even be truthful about yourself?"

Damian took another drink of the bitter brew. "I don't know, Da. But I can't let her go. I'll die without her."

"*Crivvens*, lad, you've never been prone to histrionics. What has gotten into you?"

Damian shook his head, puzzled. "If I knew I'd tell you, Da. I swear it."

"We need to figure this thing out." Dougal began punching on his keyboard. "Have you been writing?"

"Aye. The sequel's nearly done."

"Good. Now tell me. Why do you think you'll die without Suzanne?"

"I don't know. I just know that I will."

"That's no answer, lad."

"It's the only one I've got."

"You can do better than that. You're a writer. Describe to me what you're feeling."

Damian paced the room again.

"You'll wear the carpet out in here," Dougal said.

He sat down next to his father. "It's not something I can describe, because it's not something I've ever felt before. It's like…she fills a part of me that I never knew was empty. She completes me. And now that she's here, she's like an addiction. My body craves her. *Needs* her."

"Just your body, son?"

"My mind. My heart. My soul."

"I've never heard you talk of heart and soul before."

"There was never a reason to."

"I see."

"Can't you be a little more specific on your posts, Da?"

"Maybe. But I'm not willing to sacrifice your safety or sanity for this."

"I've got money, Da."

"We can't tell anyone that, lad. People will come up with stories just to get their hands on your found. You know that."

Damian sighed. "Aye."

Dougal continued to type. "I do have some good news, though."

"What's that?"

"This morning, Isabella told me she hired an electrician from Thurso to install power throughout the castle. He's coming today."

"That'll be mighty nice. Did you tell her we'd pay for it?"

"No. I didn't think you'd want her to question that. But I'll take care of it."

"Aye." Damian sniffed the air.

Fresh. Springtime. Suzanne. He smiled. He sniffed again, the whiff of testosterone unmistakable. A chill crept up the back of his neck.

"He's here now, Da."

"Who?"

"The electrician. And he's with Suzanne." Damian leaped out of his chair and ran out of the cellar room and up the stairs to the front entrance.

Suzanne stood near the doorway, her face lit by the afternoon sun streaming in. God, she was beautiful. But the smile touching her lips teased another man—an attractive man dressed in jeans and a green T-shirt, holding a tool chest.

Damian stalked forward, grabbed Suzanne by the arm, and pulled her behind his large body.

"Can I help you, friend?" Damian said to the stranger.

"I'm Clyde Ross. The electrician. I'm here to see Isabella Knight."

"This isn't Isabella." His voice was low, feral.

"I know. Suzanne was just telling me Isabella's on her way down."

"This one's mine, *friend*," Damian said. A hissing growl escaped his throat.

Clyde's blue eyes widened. Was it fear the man felt? Damian hoped so.

"Look, I was just talking to her."

Suzanne struggled out of Damian's grasp. "For God's sake, Damian, you're being ridiculous. Isabella's tied up for a minute upstairs, and I was just letting Clyde in."

"You're mine," Damian said in a savage whisper. He grabbed Suzanne's hand and whisked her away.

"Uh, excuse us," she called back to Clyde and then demanded, "What in God's name are you doing?"

When they reached the stairs, he tossed her over his shoulder and ran upward to their bedroom.

26

"What has gotten into you?" Suzanne stared into Damian's swirling irises after he tossed her onto the bed.

"You were talking to another man." Damian's voice sounded savage, bloodthirsty.

"I answered the door for Isabella." She struggled to stand, but he pushed her down. "What would you have me do? Leave the poor guy out there? It's steaming hot, and at least it's cool in this stone dungeon."

"Stone dungeon? This is my home."

"Whatever. Look, we need to get a few things straight."

"You're absolutely right, lass. I don't want you talking to other men."

"Oh, of course. No problem. While I'm at it, why don't I stay away from women, too? And dogs and cats. But can I still talk to plants, Damian? I don't know how I'd live without my botanic conversations."

"You're being sarcastic."

"Really? I hadn't noticed."

"How can you make light of this? I'm completely serious."

"Completely insane, you mean."

"Aye. Insane. You've invaded my mind. My psyche. My consciousness. I haven't written in days. Thoughts of you plague me."

"I've done nothing."

"You've captured my heart, lass. I need you."

"Please don't say I've caused you to stop writing. I couldn't live with that. You're an amazing talent. I'll leave Scotland right now if you can't write because I'm here."

"No. You can't leave."

"But you need to write."

"If you leave, I'll never write again."

"Dear Lord." She held out her arms to him, her heart aching. His eyes swirled with sadness. "Come to me."

He lay down next to her and took her in his arms. "You're my world, Suzanne. I love you."

"I want to understand you, Damian. But you can't possibly love me. You don't even know me."

He feathered butterfly kisses over her forehead and cheeks. "I know you don't understand it. I don't understand it myself. But I do love you."

"Look at you," she said. "You're amazing. You're gorgeous, you're smart, you're talented. You could have any woman in the world. Why me, Damian?"

"I wish I could explain it to you, lass, but I can't. Just don't leave me. Please don't leave me."

"I'll stay," Suzanne said, and a look of sheer bliss covered Damian's face. "For the next couple of weeks."

"Oh." His brow wrinkled.

"That's time for us to get to know each other. Then,

maybe you can come visit me in Colorado. Would you like that?"

He shook his head. "I can't leave Padraig."

"Why on earth not?"

"There are circumstances."

"What circumstances?"

"I can't say."

"Then this will never work between us. You expect me to pack up my whole life and move across the world, but you won't be honest with me. And speaking of honesty, when are you going to tell me about the injuries to your back?"

Suzanne didn't get an answer. Instead, Damian pressed his lips onto hers, nibbling across her lower lip and then her upper, teasing her with little flicks of his tongue. Although her brain told her she needed to know more about him, about why he was so possessive, why he felt this animalistic need for her, why he had been injured on his back and hands, her body knew only that she wanted him. In her mouth. In her body. In her heart.

She couldn't fight his passion, because she shared it.

Brazenly, she parted her lips and thrust her tongue into the warmth of his mouth. She kissed him with longing, intensity, lust. She poured her essence into this meeting of their mouths, making all their previous kisses meaningless. She tasted, she teased, she taunted.

Deepening the kiss, she pushed him onto his back and climbed on top of him, grinding her still-clothed pussy into his burgeoning hardness. Her body ablaze, she pushed into him while she framed his chiseled face in her hands. Every groan from him fueled her passion, every thrust of his need against her kindled her craving ache. She drove into him, against him, climbing, peaking, and then jumping into the chasm as her body exploded into a thousand flaming arrows. Higher and higher she flew, her mouth still clamped to his, her body still racked with pleasure, rapture, bliss. The climax continued, pulsing through her veins like rivers of boiling honey. She moaned into his mouth, her tongue still tangled with his.

Her best orgasm ever, and they were both still fully clothed.

She broke the kiss, panting.

"Now do you believe you're mine?" Damian's voice husky with smoke and cinders.

"Yes." Her whisper came in a breathless rasp. "I'm yours. And you're mine." She fumbled with his shirt and pulled it out of the waistband of his jeans. "Take this off."

As he did so, she unbuttoned her blouse and flung it onto the floor. Her bra followed.

Damian's gaze locked onto her nakedness. "You have the most beautiful breasts I've ever seen, Suzanne."

"Take off your pants," she said, unzipping her own. "I want you naked."

He groaned as he removed his shoes, his jeans, his boxers. His eyes locked onto hers, and her whole body ignited.

"Now, Damian," she rasped. "Take me now."

"I want to love you slowly."

"Later. Right now, I want you inside me. I need you. I don't want to wait a second longer."

"Oh God, love." He pushed her onto her back, covered her with his body, and pierced into her, stretching her exquisitely. "So sweet, so tight." His gravelly voice inflamed her. "Ah, yes. You were made for me."

Suzanne gasped with pleasure so intense, so huge. She had never been filled so completely. She locked her legs around his hips, matched him, denying him nothing. She rose to meet every thrust, forcing him more deeply into her.

"I'd stay inside you forever if I could," Damian said. He thrust and thrust.

Suzanne's skin erupted in flames, her heart bounced in her chest. "More, Damian. Harder, faster." Her breath whooshed outward in rapid puffs.

He increased his speed and pressure as he continued to plunge into her, wiggling his hips, filling every last millimeter.

She writhed underneath him, lost in ecstasy. Bliss. Rapture. Nirvana. The climax ascended higher and higher, and Damian rose onto his knees and pulled her hips to him as he pounded into her, his eyes squeezed shut and his beautiful teeth clenched. He thrust once more and his release pulsed into her as he groaned her name.

"I love you, *mo cridhe*."

27

"I'm beginning to think you're right, Damian." Suzanne snuggled closer to her lover. She buried her face in his neck and inhaled his spicy, musky fragrance.

"About what?" He kissed the top of her head.

"That we belong together."

"I never doubted it. What changed your mind?"

She smiled into his neck. "What do you think? That was incredible. That was amazing. That was…"

He pulled her on top of his body, and his soft chest hair tickled her nipples. "That, love"—he brushed his mouth over hers and nipped her bottom lip with his teeth—"was *us*."

28

Isabella hated money spells. She didn't like to use magic for her own personal gain. But Clyde Ross's estimate had come in at three thousand pounds, which was a good chunk of the inheritance Merlina had left her.

But this silly little stone castle in this bizarre little Highland village had somehow become home to her. She wanted to stay. And she needed electricity. This was the twenty-first century after all.

So she decided to do a money spell. Because she had decided to stay in Padraig, she would make it more of a "help me find gainful employment" spell. That eased her conscience a little.

But she didn't have any green candles, which were essential for a money spell, and she hadn't been able to find any in Merlina's supplies. She decided to pay a visit to the Lunar Eclipse.

Whispers and low giggles behind Suzanne's locked door kept Isabella from inviting her cousin along. Perhaps

Suzanne and Damian had finally consummated their relationship. Isabella wasn't sure how she felt about that. She prided herself on being a good judge of character. Damian was hiding something. Clearly, he cared for Suzanne, though, and that eased Isabella's discomfort somewhat. She worried more about Suzanne. Getting serious with a man so soon after her breakup with Wade couldn't lead to anything good.

Isabella left the castle, drove into Padraig and stopped at the Lunar Eclipse. Rex Donnelly busied himself behind the counter. Isabella cleared her throat.

Rex looked up. "Ah. Miss Knight. What can I be helping you with today?"

"Good afternoon, Mr. Donnelly. I need some green candles."

He smirked. "A money spell."

Isabella warmed under his gaze. "Sort of. I'm installing electricity in Merlina's castle, and as you can no doubt imagine, it's pricey."

"Pricey?"

"Expensive."

"I see."

"I've actually decided to stay here in Padraig for a while, so I'll be looking for work to help make ends meet. So it's more of an employment spell. I don't believe in getting something for nothing."

"You're a pure white witch, then."

"Yes. I pride myself on it."

Rex stepped out from behind the counter and led Isabella to the candle display. "Here we are, then."

Isabella selected her candles. "These will do nicely. Thank you, Mr. Donnelly."

"Please, lass, call me Rex. I like to be on a first name basis with my employees."

"Your employees?" Isabella smiled and handed back the candles. "I guess I won't be needing these."

29

"I'm afraid I wasn't thinking." Damian kissed the fleshy mound of Suzanne's breast.

"Hmmm?" Her eyes remained shut, and she looked delectable. Good enough to eat. Again.

"I'm sorry. I didn't use a condom." He couldn't bring himself to care. He didn't have any diseases, and he instinctively knew she didn't either. He could tell from her scent. And pregnancy wasn't a problem. He couldn't get her pregnant. It wasn't the right time. He wasn't sure how he knew that, but he did, and he accepted it without question.

Although part of him wished he had gotten her pregnant. He wanted her soft belly to swell with his child. The image of it made him want to howl. But he couldn't let it happen. He couldn't risk creating another creature like himself. They would never have children. His eyes misted. He wanted Suzanne to bear his child. He wanted it so badly it hurt.

Fate was cruel.

"Mmm," she murmured again. "S'okay. I'm on the pill."

She breathed in deeply and then jolted upward. "What? Oh my God."

"What is it?"

"I hardly know you. You don't have anything *catching*, do you?"

He chuckled. "Of course not. I'm hardly promiscuous, and I've always used protection in the past. And you're fine, too."

She sighed, her breath a sweet whisper against his chest. "Thank God. Yes, I'm fine, too." Her chin jerked upward again. "How do you know I'm fine?"

"I know you, love. You wouldn't have let me make love to you if you had any doubts."

"Mmm. True enough." She sighed again, and he felt her body loosen. "How do you know me so well?"

"Because you're mine."

The curve of her lips against his chest contented him. How had he lived for thirty-five years without her?

"Feel like a shower?" she asked.

"With you?"

"Of course with me." She raised her gaze, and her foggy eyes met his. Her brows lifted and she smiled, dimples dancing on her cheeks. "And not a cold one, either."

"Later." He pushed her onto her back and trapped her beneath him. "I want to eat first."

"Is there anything in the kitchen?"

"Not what I had in mind."

He brushed her mouth with his, trailed kisses down her breasts, her belly, her thighs, and then he spread her legs. His pulse raced at the sight of her glistening folds. God, she was beautiful. So perfectly formed, so beautifully pink. Still swollen and wet for him. A feast.

He dived in, her creamy taste filling his senses. She arched into him and moaned his name.

He lifted his head and gazed at her perfect body, shiny with perspiration. "I love how you say my name, Suzanne. Say it again."

"Damian," she purred. "I love what you do to me. Damian. My Damian."

His name had never sounded sweeter. He lowered his head and licked her in long, smooth strokes of his tongue. Oh yes, this was going to be a pleasant afternoon. He licked and tugged, slipped two fingers inside her as her walls clenched around him. He sucked and sucked, launching her into another climax, and then another. He drove her relentlessly, determined to prove to her what he already knew.

She was his.

He was hers.

Fate.

Forever.

When she screamed his name, he crawled upward and plunged inside her. "Mine," he said against her lips. "Suzanne. Mine."

30

"How am I supposed to get this done if you keep touching me *there?*" Suzanne squirmed away from Damian's roving hands and looked through the dark pantry for something she could throw together for dinner.

"Sorry, love, you're just too tempting a morsel to ignore."

He cupped her breast and thumbed her nipple through her tank top. She hadn't bothered with a bra, and his fondling sent shivers straight to her core.

She turned into his arms and looked into his hazel eyes, his gaze burning into her. "When you look at me like that, I..."

"You what?"

"I can't think." She pushed him away. "I told you I'd make you something to eat, and I intend to do it. I'm a great cook. I want to cook for you." God, she wanted to cook for him. For her man. "But you need to stop touching me."

He grinned at her. "Never." He pulled her back into his embrace and kissed the spot below her ear that made her swoon. "I think about you all the time. I can barely breathe when you're near me. I dream of holding you, of you making love to me with that beautiful body." He nipped her earlobe. "I can't be in the same room with you and not touch you."

"Then how am I supposed to fix your dinner?"

"Can't I just crawl into your skin while you work?"

She chuckled against his shadowed jaw. "Oh, I love the thought of that... But no." She pulled away. "You. Sit." She pointed to a chair at the worktable. "There."

"Aye, love." He saluted and sat down. And promptly pulled her into his lap and started kissing her again.

"You're incorrigible, Damian MacGowan." But she returned his kiss. How could she not? "You have me all tied up in knots." Her words came out in a breathless rasp. "I don't know which way is up when we're together. You make me feel things I'm not ready to feel yet. But..."

"Hmm? What love?"

"It feels so right."

"Aye." He kissed her again. Hard. Deep.

"Did you two ever think of getting a room?"

Suzanne broke the kiss upon hearing Isabella's voice. "Good one, Bell. Like a room would stop you."

Damian's chuckle tickled Suzanne's neck.

"Damian and I were going to have some dinner. I've been bragging about my culinary skills."

"Suze is a great cook," Isabella agreed.

"Of course, I'm used to a gas range and a microwave. This"—she gestured to the wood stove—"will be a challenge."

"Tonight you don't need to cook. I brought dinner." Isabella held up a shopping bag. "I stopped by the Pit, and Gwennie made me some roast beef sandwiches and pasta salad, and then I stopped off for a little something extra." She pulled out a bottle of champagne. "To celebrate."

"What are we celebrating?" Suzanne asked.

"My new job, for one. I'm working at the Lunar Eclipse."

"With the—" Suzanne clamped her mouth shut. She had almost said vampire.

"Rex offered me the work. Isn't that great? What a perfect job for me."

"So you're staying in Padraig, then?" This from Damian.

"Yeah. And I'm trying to talk Suze into staying, too. Maybe you can exert some influence with her."

Damian smiled. "Sure and I'll try, lass."

"Try hard," Isabella said. "I need her."

"As do I."

This in a whisper, for Suzanne's ears only. Heat ribboned through her.

"Let me help you." Suzanne left Damian's lap and started to take food out of the bag. "What else are we celebrating?"

"The return to the twenty-first century. Our electricity should be installed within a week." She turned to Damian. "I have you and your father to thank for keeping the costs down. I had no idea the castle was already tapped into the line."

"Keeping costs down?" Suzanne wrinkled her brow.

"Yeah. Three thousand pounds. That includes all appliances and a few gas lines as well. It's a lot, but it would have been twice as much if he had to hook us all the way up. Your friend there"—she nodded to Damian—"evidently installed power in the cellar several years ago."

Suzanne turned to Damian with a questioning gaze.

"Aye, Suzanne. For my work."

"I can't believe Merlina allowed it," Isabella said.

"Da and I never told her. I've a feeling she knew, but kept quiet," he said. "She knew my, er, situation, so she knew Da and I needed the power. She kept one eye shut."

Suzanne quickly changed the subject. "I don't know about you two, but I'm famished. Shall we see what Gwennie cooked up for us?"

"It's no lasagna à la Suzanne, but I'm sure it'll do," Isabella said. "But first, a toast." She unwrapped the foil from the champagne bottle and uncorked it. "Where's your father, Damian? I'd like him to join us." She pulled several flutes from a cupboard and poured the sparkling wine.

"I'm right here, lass," Dougal said from the doorway. "Did I hear you'll be staying in bonny Padraig?"

"Yes," Isabella said, "if you'll have me."

"It's your castle. Perhaps Damian and I should be asking if you'll have us?" He smiled, and his friendly eyes crinkled.

"Oh, of course. This is your home. I want you to stay. Both of you."

"Then we'd be obliged. And we'll pay whatever rent you think is fair."

"Oh, that's not necessary. Just keep taking care of the place. That's all I need."

"Mighty generous of you lass, but I assure you we're fully capable of—"

"I won't hear of it," Isabella said. "Besides, I just got a job today. At the Lunar Eclipse."

"Congratulations, then." Dougal raised his glass of champagne.

"Thank you. And maybe you and your son can help me convince my cousin to stay here as well."

"We'll certainly try, won't we, lad?" Dougal winked at his son.

Damian stood behind Suzanne and pulled her body into his. "Aye. We will at that."

Suzanne smiled as she felt the tickle of his lips on her neck.

"Oh, by the way," Isabella said to Dougal, "Clyde needs to turn off the power to your office in the cellar first thing in the morning. It'll be off for a few days until he gets the whole place up and running."

"I've already logged off for the night," Dougal said. "It shouldn't be a problem."

Isabella turned to Damian. "I hope this doesn't cause you any problems."

Damian lifted his lips from Suzanne's neck, his husky voice a sweet caress on her skin. "I'm sure I'll find ways to pass the time, lass." He brushed his lips against her neck again. "*Mo leannan.*"

Mo leannan. My lover, he'd called her.

Suzanne couldn't help herself. Right in front of Isabella and Dougal, she turned around in Damian's arms, facing him, and captured his beautiful lips with her own.

He lifted her off her feet, and she instinctively wrapped her legs around his waist. He broke the kiss.

"Save us some dinner." He returned his mouth to hers as he walked out of the kitchen and toward the stairs.

31

Rohricht Telikov yawned. He had just come in from a night run, and his body ached from fatigue.

"Come to bed, Rohr," called his wife.

"A few minutes, *yogodka*," he said. "I need to check the dates on some shipments."

"I'm hungry," she said, a sexy whine in her voice.

He smiled. His Elena was insatiable, just the way he liked her. "I'll take care of you. It won't be long."

He logged on to the Internet and decided to quickly check his e-mail before tackling the shipments. *Hmm. A new message.* He didn't recognize the name of the sender—Wolfman243. The short message read: "Saw this post and thought it might interest you."

Rohricht clicked on the link.

Damn.

32

"They're beautiful together, aren't they?"

Isabella nodded to Dougal as they sat on the back terrace and watched Suzanne and Damian romping in the courtyard. She chased him, pounced on him. But he was too quick for her. Within seconds, he had her on her back in the grass, and then he was on top of her, kissing her.

"I've never seen Damian so happy. I can't begin to think what he'll go through when she leaves."

"She may still decide to stay," Isabella said. "They've been inseparable for nearly four weeks. And now that we have power and all..." She sighed. "I know Clyde took longer than expected, but isn't it great to have electric light?"

"Aye, lass. But the bloke did something to my system downstairs. I haven't been able to log on since the power's been back up."

"Hmm. Did you ask Clyde about it?"

"Aye. He's says I need some newfangled cable or some

such nonsense. He's coming tomorrow to install it." Dougal chuckled. "If Merlina could see us now."

Isabella shook her head. "I know next to nothing about Merlina. I wish I'd had the chance to get to know her."

"She was a remarkable woman." Dougal closed his eyes. "Remarkable. Very kind and giving. Loving. Damian was usually writing, so Merlina and I would bring a glass of wine out here during the warmer evenings and talk. She told me all about you. She was like a mother to Damian. She doted on him. Couldn't do enough for him. I'll always love her for that."

"What happened to Damian's mother?"

"My wife, you mean?"

"Yeah."

"I've never been married. Damian's not my natural son."

"Oh." Isabella took a sip of her chardonnay. "I had no idea."

"Hasn't Damian told Suzanne?"

"If he has, she hasn't told me."

"It's a bit of a sad story, you see. Damian was abandoned as a wee bairn. I found him in an alley in Glasgow, nearly starved."

Isabella's hands whipped to her mouth. "That's horrible!"

"Aye. Normally, I would have taken him to the authorities, but...well, this will sound very strange to you."

"I'm a witch, Dougal. Nothing sounds strange to me."

"Aye. Maybe you will understand. Merlina did." He cleared his throat. "The truth is, when I picked up the babe, he seemed to speak to me. Not in words, of course. But he seemed to say that I was his destiny. That he knew I would take care of him. That he would die otherwise. At that moment, he became my son."

Isabella nodded. "I do understand. Sometimes, we just know."

"Aye. So I brought him here to Padraig. I'd been a wanderer up until then. I'd had a bad few years. My lassie, my love, had passed on, and Damian gave me a reason to live again. I hadn't worked in a while, but I knew I had to find some way to provide for my bairn. I knocked on Merlina's door one night, and as you Yanks say, the rest is history."

"Did you ever try to find Damian's family?"

"I had good intentions, I did. But the lad crept into my heart so quickly. I would never have been able to give him up. And anyone who'd leave a newborn babe in an alley didn't deserve him, as far as I was concerned."

Isabella nodded. "I'd agree. You're no doubt the best thing that ever happened to him."

Dougal smiled and shook his head. "Not I, lass." He gestured toward the two young lovers laughing together on the grass. "The best thing to ever happen to him is your cousin."

33

Damian rose from the bed, the light of dawn streaking in through the window. Beautiful, his Padraig. The fresh hilly countryside. He turned toward the bed. The beauty of his village paled next to his Suzanne. Her curvy body lay tangled in the sheets. Memories of their night of lovemaking assaulted his senses. The warm glow of her skin, like silk under his fingers. The heady scent of her shiny hair, veiling him as she lay on top of him, her mouth on his. The creamy taste of her cunt on his tongue. The caress of her eyes as she gazed at his body. The sweet tightness of her walls around his cock. Her sexy laugh. His name dripping from her lips, like a hot surging whisper against his flesh.

He was hard for her again. He would never get enough of her. He longed to wake her and plunge into her body. But the peaceful aura of her sleeping body overpowered his need. She was an angel. His angel. He couldn't disturb her.

He smiled as he thought about the day ahead of them.

They would ride the Harley into Thurso. She had asked him to take her to get a tattoo. Her first. She wanted a wolf, like his but smaller, on her lower back.

And he had a surprise in store for her. He was going to have her name tattooed on his arm. He'd be marked forever. Hers. Always. He felt like howling his possession to the world.

His loins tightened as she stirred. Her crimson lips curled upward slightly and she sighed, her eyes still closed. "Mmm. Damian."

He sat down on the bed. "I'm here, *mo leannan*." He feathered his fingers over her satiny cheek.

"Mmm," she said again and rolled toward him. "Love me."

"I do, Suzanne."

She smiled, her dimples appearing on her beautiful cheeks, and his heart leaped.

Unable to stop himself, he leaned down and brushed his lips over hers. "*Mo leannan*," he whispered.

"*Mo leannan*," she whispered back. "Love me, Damian."

He covered her body with his, nudged her thighs open, and settled between them. "Open your eyes, *mo leannan*, and look at me."

Her lashes fluttered, and Damian drowned in the night fog, the golden sparks. So beautiful. He pressed his lips to hers in a gentle kiss. He trailed his mouth down her neck and shoulders, over the delicious mounds of her breasts, until he flicked his tongue over one cherry red nipple. Suzanne arched beneath him, murmuring the sexy sounds he loved. He licked her again and then captured the swollen bud between his teeth and tugged gently. He never tired of the sugary taste of her nipples. He laved and sucked, fueled by her sexy moans.

"So beautiful," he murmured. "All mine."

He turned to her other nipple and lavished it with attention while one hand reached between her legs. "Wet, *mo leannan*. Wet for me."

"For you," she whispered as her hips gyrated up and down against his searching fingers.

He slid two inside her and rubbed, finding the spot that drove her over the edge.

"Yes," she whispered. "Just like that."

He tore his lips from her nipple and found her mouth, sweet as blueberry wine, and plunged his cock into her body. "Ah," he groaned. Each time was better than the last. Each time, she was a more perfect fit. He thrust only twice before they both toppled into rapture together, climaxing in tandem, their spasms in total synchrony.

Mine.

Mine.

Mine.

Later, he wrapped her in his arms and whispered into her ear. "Each time, I want you more, *mo leannan*. We've just made love, and already I'm wanting to touch you again, feel your heart beat against my flesh, bury myself inside your warmth. I can't get enough of you. Your taste. Your smell. Why, *mo leannan*? Why is it like this?"

"I don't know," she murmured into his shoulder.

"I knew from the first moment that you were mine," he said, "but I never imagined it would be like this. Loving you." He inhaled the fresh scent of her hair. "Loving you is a gift, Suzanne. You're my heart, my soul. You're everything."

"Mmm."

Her voice hummed against his throat and her breathing

became shallower, indicating sleep. He pulled her closer to his body.

My heart. My soul. My love.

34

Markus opened the door and entered. For three weeks, he had kept the young American imprisoned in an old abandoned cottage on the outskirts of town. Markus had fed the man well, beef and venison, bloody rare of course, with potatoes and cabbage and lots and lots of Guinness. The red meat increased the iron and testosterone in the blood, making it more potent. The Guinness, well, that just made it taste even better. The American—Wade was his name—hadn't complained. Markus kept him comfortable, with a four-poster bed, a flat-screen TV, and one of those Japanese video game consoles. Thanks to Markus's mind control, Wade thought he had lost his way in the Highlands and had become ill. Good Samaritan Markus had found him and cared for him in the cottage until he could resume his travel.

Markus came early in the morning, before first light, and after dusk, to feed from Wade. He couldn't keep the American much longer. Soon, someone would come looking for him. He had considered releasing him for the last several days. But then the bloodlust would hit, and faced with the hunger for Wade's androgen-laced plasma, he hadn't been able to discharge his prey. What the hell? Wade seemed perfectly content to lounge in his Highland bungalow, watching TV and playing something called Final Fantasy.

Damned lazy Americans. No wonder the majority of them were overweight.

Not this one, though, and not that stacked little chippie Rex had thrown him a few weeks ago either. Markus would have loved a taste of her. Just thinking about that night consumed him with wrath. He had a score to settle with Damian MacGowan, *Voldlak* or not.

Aye. Female. It was time to let Wade go. Because as much as he savored the male's blood, Markus couldn't find satiation of another nature with him. He had no sexual hunger for males. Markus was ready for the sweet tang of a female. In more ways than one.

Markus's gums stung as his fangs elongated, his salivary glands activated. One more taste.

He approached the bed where the American lay, still slumbering. Markus sat down on the bed next to him and touched his cheek to keep him asleep. While he sometimes enjoyed tormenting his prey, feeding from their fear and screams, he had grown tired of it with Wade. He wanted a quick drink. Then he'd wake the man and let him go.

With wide eyes, he sank his teeth into the man's neck and sucked. As the intoxicating liquid oozed down his throat, Wade's strength and masculinity flowed into Markus. He sated himself, careful not to take more than a cup. Wade needed his strength to leave later today. He carefully licked the wounds closed and wiped his mouth. Then he shook the sleeping man.

"Friend," he said, "how are you feeling today?"

Wade opened his eyes and struggled to sit up, clearly a bit weak from the blood loss. "All right, I guess. You?"

"Never better. Your color's back to normal, and your temperature down. Sure and I'm thinking you can be on your way today. Where are you headed?"

"A castle outside Padraig. My fiancée's cousin inherited it."

"Not the O'Day place?" *MacGowan.*

"Don't know. The new owner's name is Isabella Knight."

"Doesn't ring a bell."

"My fiancée's name is Suzanne Wood."

"What's she look like, mate?"

"Brown hair, gray eyes." Wade grinned coltishly. "Stacked."

Markus chuckled. "Sounds like my kind of woman." And remarkably like the woman he had almost tasted a few weeks ago, until Damian MacGowan had interfered.

Maybe...

"I can show you to the O'Day place, friend." Markus stood and looked out the window. "It's not far from here. I'll take you there after sundown."

"Why not sooner?"

Because I'll incinerate in the sun. "Work, mate. But I'll be back."

He left the cottage and went to his car parked in the drive. As he grasped the car door handle, a gust of icy wind sliced into his back, pelting his skin with freezing glass shards.

Icy wind? In midsummer? Glass shards?

He turned to face long hair even paler than his own falling from a widow's peak around an eerily beautiful face. Glowing crimson eyes burned into Markus's flesh.

"Morning, Da."

35

The pale man extended one long manicured finger to Markus's chin and wiped away a small speck of blood. "Been keeping blood slaves again, lad?"

"Maybe I just cut myself shaving."

"I know you better than that."

Markus scoffed. "You don't know me at all. And I haven't hurt him. I'm letting him go tonight."

"Do you think I give a damn if you hurt him?" The demonic guffaw chilled the blood that rushed through Markus's veins. "I've never understood your taste for male blood, boy."

"You don't understand my taste for blood period, Da."

"Aye. 'Twas your mother's curse, the bloodlust."

"'Twas *your* curse, Da. Mum lives on sheep's blood. But the demon in me craves it fresh, from humans."

"Don't blame me. I can't stand the stuff. It's thick and sticky and cakes my throat." Samael twisted his full lips into a churlish grin as his evil slithered over Markus, starting at his toes and snaking all the way to the top of his head.

"For someone who hates blood, you've shed your share of it."

"Aye." Samael leered. "As have you, *son*."

"'Twasn't my fault. 'Twas the bloodlust. I lost control."

"You shouldn't feel remorse. That's your mother's influence." Samael's lips curved upward again.

Markus shuddered. Evil. Pure evil.

"How is dear Viveca?"

"Mum's fine. You stay away from her."

"Still a beauty, I bet."

"I said stay away."

"There's never been another like her, you know. She was one in a million. And I do mean a million. The only one worthy to nurture my seed. You're my only progeny, lad. You should be proud."

"Proud that I'm half demon? Proud that I need to drink blood from living humans to survive? I'm nothing like you."

"Ah, you're more like me than you want to admit. You suffer not only the bloodlust, but the lust for the kill. You've killed before."

The icy coldness of Samael's voice slid over Markus's body like freezing rain.

"They were accidents." Markus shook his head. "I took too much, is all."

"And 'twas only a few weeks ago that you desired to kill a man, was it not?"

Markus's blood froze. "How did you know that?"

"You're part of me. I feel what you feel."

Markus couldn't deny it. "Aye, Da. I wanted to kill."

"What was it about this man that inspired the lust, lad?"

"He was *Voldlak*."

"Ah." Samael's long pale hair snaked in coils as he nodded his head. "A blood wolf. A vampire's worst nightmare. So they do exist after all."

"Aye."

"Then let's get him, lad. Let's get him."

36

"Damian," Suzanne said. "Come see it. It's gorgeous."

Damian smiled and peeked under her blouse in the back. "Aye, *mo leannan*. Very nice." His eyes smiled into hers. "Do you want to see mine?"

"Yours?"

"Aye." He rolled up the sleeve of his shirt. Suzanne gasped, her eyes wide. On his upper arm, in old English script, was her name entwined around a vermillion heart.

"Damian?"

"Do you like it, *mo leannan*?"

"I don't know what to say."

"Say you like it." Damian wrapped his arms around her and whispered in her ear. "Say you'll get one like it someday. For me."

Suzanne shrugged out of his hold. She was leaving in less than a week. He knew that. "Damian, let's take care of the bill, okay? Then we'll talk. What do I owe you, Seamus?"

"I took care of it."

"Oh." Of course, he would have. He was richer than God. And domineering. "I guess we're done here."

She walked out the door and headed for the Harley, which was parked in the back. Damian placed a hand on her shoulder, and she turned around to face him. His green eyes were shadowed.

"Hey," she said.

"I thought you'd like it, *mo leannan*. I wanted you to know that I'm yours. Forever."

"You're so sweet, Damian. So wonderful."

His face brightened. "You do like it, then?"

"I love it. Really. I just... It's too soon for forever. We both know that."

"Just what did you think I meant when I said *you're mine*, Suzanne?"

"I—"

"And what exactly did you mean when you said I was yours? Did you mean for the next few weeks? Because you know damn well that's not what I meant."

"Let's not snipe at each other."

"Snipe?"

"Argue. Fight."

"Fine. No arguing. You're mine, and I'm yours, and that's that."

"Damian, I leave in less than a week."

"You're staying."

"Nothing has changed. I have a job. A family. A life back home."

"You're life is here now. With me."

"I care very much for you, but—"

"I love you. You know that."

"You *think* you love me."

"Don't ever tell me what I think," he said through clenched teeth. "I know damn well that I love you."

Suzanne shook her head. "I'm sorry. It's too soon for me. I care for you very deeply. But love? I'm not sure I even know what love is anymore."

"So these past weeks have meant nothing to you? Our time together? Our lovemaking?"

"Oh Damian, it's meant everything to me. But nothing has changed."

"How can you say that?"

"Because. Oh, I don't know."

"I love you. I won't let you leave me."

"Let's not argue here." She reached for his cheek. His skin was icy to her touch. "Are you hungry? Shall we have lunch?"

He handed her helmet to her. "I can't eat right now. Let's head back to Padraig."

"But I thought we were going to visit the docks after lunch."

"Change of plans." He fastened his helmet and sat down on the Harley. He turned the key and revved the engine.

Suzanne sat down behind him and wrapped her arms around his waist. She leaned into him and pressed her breasts into his back. The usual comfort she felt in this position now gone, she felt only coldness from Damian. She had hurt him. The last thing she ever wanted to do.

But it had been inevitable. This fixation he had with her would end at some point. Of that, she was certain. After all, Wade had stopped loving her after five years. She steeled herself against the coming torture. She couldn't handle another break up. Better to keep Damian at arm's length for the rest of her stay. She eased away from his body and tried to enjoy the ride. But where before, the bike had held fascination, fun, daring, it now held only torment. The summer wind in her hair, against her skin, had lost its appeal.

When they arrived at the castle, Damian lifted her from the bike and unsnapped her helmet. But instead of the passionate kiss she usually got when their heads were free of the armor, he only looked at her sadly. She reached for him, but he pushed her hand away.

"Not now," he said. "I can't."

"I understand," she whispered, willing the tears not to fall. She hurried into the castle.

"Suze." Isabella rose when Suzanne entered the front room. "You have company."

"What?"

A man sat on one of the sofas, his back to Suzanne. He looked remarkably like...

"Wade?"

Her skin froze as the auburn-haired man stood and turned toward her.

"Hi, Suzie."

"What are you doing here?"

"I needed to see you," he said. Then, "Who's that?"

Suzanne grabbed Damian's hand. "This is Damian MacGowan. He lives here. He's the caretaker's son." She wanted to add more. He was so much more than that. But what could she say? Boyfriend sounded so infantile. Friend would be an insult. Lover? The day Suzanne Wood introduced any man as her lover was the day that pigs would fly to the moon. Her heart lurched. After today, they might not be lovers anymore anyway.

Wade held out his hand. "Wade Stallworth. Suzanne's fiancé."

Damian's eyes grew darker, and the ominous swirling began.

"Ex-fiancé," she said.

Suzanne sensed Damian's hesitation, but he took Wade's hand in a masculine grasp. He inhaled and then dropped Wade's hand as though it were a hot coal.

Wade turned to Suzanne. "I need to talk to you. Can you get away for a few hours? Maybe for a late lunch?"

She had nothing to say to Wade, but he had come all this way to see her. It wouldn't hurt to see what he wanted.

"Uh, sure, I suppose I could go with you."

Damian grabbed her arm. "Don't go."

"Now you want to be with me?"

"It has nothing to do with us. Just don't go. Please."

"Could you excuse us for a few minutes?" Suzanne said to Wade.

She led Damian to the kitchen.

"What's going on now?"

"Don't go with him," Damian said.

"I swear I have no feelings for him at all, okay? But he came all this way to see me. Surely I owe him a few hours of my time."

"You owe him nothing. Don't go. It doesn't feel right."

"What?"

"I can't explain it any better than that."

"More of your feelings? Like how you and I are destined to be together? You can't explain why, and I'm just supposed to accept what you say?"

"Aye."

Suzanne shook her head. "I don't work that way, Damian. I'm a lawyer. I need logic. Reasoning."

"Don't go." His eyes pleaded with her. They were clouded

and angry. But underneath the wrath was sadness. Damian was in pain. She reached for him, but he pulled away. "Trust me. Don't go."

"I do trust you. I do. But where is the harm?"

"I can't say."

"I'm sorry, Damian, but I'm going. I spent five years of my life with Wade, and he traveled across the world to see me. The least I can do is find out what he wants." Unable to look at his shrouded eyes again, she turned and walked out.

"Let's go," she said to Wade.

"So where's a good place to eat around here?" Wade asked once they were on the road in his rented Jaguar.

"Honestly, I haven't eaten in Padraig much. Mostly, Damian and I have gone to Thurso. There are some fabulous places there."

"You and Damian?"

"Yeah."

"Are you two together?"

"Yeah. Sort of." But maybe not any longer. She looked at her ex-fiancé. He was handsome, no doubt, and more refined as compared to Damian's ruggedness. Manicured fingernails, side burns trimmed just so. Damian's soft unruly waves were so much nicer.

"So." He cleared his throat. "You're with that Damian fellow."

"Yeah. We've spent a lot of time together."

"Then you and I definitely need to talk now."

"Why?"

"Gloriana and I broke up."

"Who's Gloriana?" Suzanne chuckled as she realized she knew. "The slut from your office who you dumped me for?"

"It was a foolish mistake."

"A mistake? As I recall, you told me you were soul mates, Wade."

"My only soul mate is sitting next to me. You, Suzanne."

"Me? That's a laugh."

"Yes. You. I should never have let you go."

She sighed. "But you did."

"And I've paid for it every day since then."

"While you were in bed with Gloriana?" Suzanne scoffed. "Yeah, that's paying all right."

"She was after my money."

She rolled her eyes. "Big surprise there."

"You never cared about my money."

"No, I didn't."

"You loved me."

"Once. Or I thought I did."

"Come on, Suzie. You loved me. I want you back."

Suzanne jerked her head backward at the surprise of his words. "Damn, Wade. Don't do that again. You'll give me whiplash."

"I'm serious."

Suzanne didn't scoff, didn't laugh. She just slowly shook her head. "You're serious. You want me. Hairy old Suzanne, who couldn't have an orgasm with you?"

"You couldn't?"

"Nope. Never. But it turns out, I wasn't the problem. Because Damian had no trouble giving me one."

"So you're sleeping with him."

"I sure am."

"What's that mick got that I haven't?"

"Me."

Suzanne stared at the rolling Highland hills as they sped past. So true. Damian had her. Wade meant nothing to her anymore. She closed her eyes and conjured her lover's face in her mind's eye. His beautiful silky hair falling in waves around his handsome face. His perfectly chiseled nose and chin, the scraping of night beard against his jaw line. Those full, luscious lips that knew exactly how to kiss her. And his eyes. His amazing, swirling, jaded cognac eyes.

Eyes she had last seen laced with pain. Pain she had caused.

"Turn around, Wade."

"Pardon me?"

"I said turn around. I want to go home."

"Home? To Colorado?"

"No. To the castle. To Damian."

"You mean we can't even talk about getting back together?"

"I'm sorry. But no. You blew it, Wade. And I want to be with Damian. So turn around."

"I can't."

"I want to be with Damian. I need to be with Damian. So don't tell me you can't turn around. We're over."

"I can't turn around, Suzanne."

Suzanne stared at Wade as he pulled into a long driveway toward a small cottage. His eyes were troubled. They looked *vacant*. "What the..."

Wade brought the Jaguar to a stop and pulled her out of the car. "I'm sorry," he said.

"Wade?"

"I can't help myself. For whatever it's worth, I did come here to get back together with you. I made a huge mistake letting you go. You deserve the best. Not..."

"Not what?"

Two figures approached them. "Not us, I imagine is what the good lad wants to say."

Suzanne's spine tingled at the sudden chilliness. The voice came from a tall blond man with hair pale as moonlight. And eyes the color of blood.

His companion seemed familiar to Suzanne. Blond hair tied in a low ponytail, emerald green eyes. It was him. From that first night. Her skin crawled as he moved toward her and inhaled.

"*Voldlak*," he said. "The bastard's fucked you in the last"—he inhaled again—"six hours, I'd say."

"You got your nose from your mother, lad," the other said.

"Wade?" Suzanne's voice cracked. Her pulse raced. Wade wouldn't let them hurt her. Would he?

"We've no more use for you," the red-eyed man said to Wade. He cupped Wade's face in long, slender hands. "You'll take your car and luggage and go to the airport. You'll book the next flight home. You had a great holiday in the Highlands."

"Right, right." Wade's eyes relaxed. "It was great to see you, Suzie. I've got a flight to catch."

"Wade, no!" Suzanne screamed. "Don't leave me here!"

"I'll give my best to your folks. See you when you get home."

"Wade!"

Suzanne ached as he drove away. She looked up. The ponytailed blond hovered over her and moved toward her neck. He opened his mouth and fangs appeared.

Suzanne's heart raced as her mind let go. Blackness swirled and enveloped her, until she could no longer see the fanged smile of her captor. The last sound she heard was her own body hitting the ground with a thud.

37

"She's gone, Da."

Dougal turned from his computer. "That blasted cable isn't working." He looked at his son's eyes. "Lad?"

"She's gone."

"Suzie?"

"Aye. She left with him."

"With who, Damian? What are you talking about?"

"Her fiancé. He came for her. I asked her not to go, but she did."

"Not back to America?"

"No. Out to lunch."

Dougal smiled, shaking his head. "*Crivvens*, lad, you had me worried there a minute. So she went out to lunch. So what? The lass loves *you*, Damian. No one else."

Damian shook his head, his heart breaking. "She doesn't, Da."

"I've watched the two of you together for the past weeks. She loves you, lad. I'm sure of it."

"I thought she might. I thought she could. But..." He shook his head. "It's over. And I don't know how I'll go on."

"You'll go on, lad. But you won't have to. She's gone to lunch, for Christ's sake. She hasn't left the country."

"I asked her not to go with him. But she left anyway."

"She's a strong, independent woman. She doesn't take well to orders. You must know that by now."

"Aye. But I sensed danger for her. I asked her to stay."

"Did you tell her there was danger?"

"I told her it didn't feel right. But I couldn't tell her anything else because I didn't *know* anything else. She left anyway."

"She's known the other lad for years. Sure and she didn't think there was any danger."

"She should have trusted me."

"Aye. Perhaps. But Damian lad, you haven't trusted her."

"I trust her."

"Not with your darkest secret."

Damian raked his fingers through his tousled hair. Dougal was right. And the full moon was only days away. He hadn't forgotten. He had just chosen to ignore it for as long as he could. With Suzanne, he had almost felt normal. Whole. A man, instead of a beast.

"Do you really think there's danger?" Dougal asked.

"Aye. I was right the last time."

"Then, lad, why are you still here?"

Right. Damian nodded. Suzanne may not love him, but he loved her. More than his own life. And he sensed something off with Wade. He turned to speak to his father, but then doubled over, and a gnashing pain sliced through his side. In his mind, Suzanne screamed for him.

"Lad!" Dougal rushed toward him.

"She's in trouble. She needs me. Auugh!" The pain sliced into him again. "Just like that first night." His eyes prickled as his irises swirled. The change always began in his eyes.

"Lad—" Dougal brushed his son's arm. Damian looked down at the thickening hair. "Concentrate. Don't let the animal take you. You've been here before. She needs you. Damian—the man."

"Aye."

"Come on. I'll take you."

"No, Da. I have to go to her myself. She's mine to care for. I've let her down. But never again, Da. Never again."

"I want to help you, son."

"No!" Damian roared, and the wolf fought to escape the confines of his skin. He backed off. "I'm sorry, Da. But I can't be worried about you and her. Please, stay here."

Damian closed his eyes and tried desperately to keep the wolf at bay. He had never changed without a full moon, but since Suzanne had come into his life, it had almost happened twice now. She needed him whole. She may not love him, but she was still his. And he would protect her.

He raced upstairs and outside and revved up his Harley. As the first night, he sensed her presence and her fear. It exploded in the depths of his bowels, his marrow. He kicked the engine into gear, and the bike screamed into the afternoon.

38

Isabella was surprised to find the Lunar Eclipse vacant when she walked in for her afternoon shift. "Rex?"

No response.

The store was clearly open for business, and several customers browsed. She answered a few questions for them and rang up some purchases. When the store emptied, she went to look for Rex. She hadn't known him long, but he seemed a serious businessman who wouldn't leave his store wide open and unattended without a good reason.

She searched the back and the storeroom.

No Rex.

One door remained closed. The door that led to his basement flat.

She took a deep breath and knocked. When no response came, she opened the door.

Slowly, she walked down the winding stairs. At the bottom was another door. She knocked again.

Nothing.

Tentatively, she opened the door. "Rex?" She walked into a short hallway. "Rex? It's me. Isabella. Where are you?"

"I'm in here, lass," he said. "My study."

"Oh. I'm sorry to bother you, but why did you leave the store? Can I come in?"

"Sure. Second door on the right."

He sat before a computer, busily tapping on the keyboard. Boxes of files littered the room, and papers lay scattered everywhere. Only inches of the beige carpeting were visible.

"Is everything okay?" Isabella asked.

"No, lass, I'm afraid not. My nephew, you see. He's missing."

"Oh. I'm sorry. Is he quite young?"

"No. A grown man. But my sister and I are very close, and she's beside herself. I've quite a bad feeling myself."

"Why?"

"It seems he has the strange idea that—" Rex stopped in mid-sentence. "I cannot really talk about it. Family confidences, you know."

Isabella nodded. "I understand. I'll just get back up to the store. Unless..." She eyed the mess. "You'd like some help down here?"

"Ah, lass." Rex stretched his arms over his head. "It's been a long day for me. Would it trouble you very much if I asked you to mind the store yourself this afternoon?"

"No. I don't mind."

"You're a fine lass, Isabella. I don't know what I'd do without you." He stretched again, yawning this time. "I could use a stiff Guinness."

"I'll get it for you," Isabella said. She walked to the kitchen, which she had noticed on her way in.

As Isabella opened the refrigerator, Rex came running out of the office.

"Isabella, no!"

But it was too late. Scattered among the bottles of Guinness were white butchers' bags. Sheep's blood. Isabella gasped as her nerves tightened and her stomach cramped. Nausea overtook her.

"Oh, lass." Rex held out his hand to her.

"My God." Isabella choked out the works. "So it's true."

"Merlina should have told you."

"She did. Only not in so many words. I never met her, you know." Isabella swallowed the lump in her throat. "But I didn't believe it."

"Can't say I blame you. Yanks usually don't believe it. There aren't many of us in the States. Not many in Europe anymore, either, for that matter. Those of us who have chosen to stay have settled here. In Padraig. Most are in Romania and Hungary. Some in Russia."

Isabella stared at the white packets. "You drink blood."

"Aye. Unnatural to you, I understand. But to us, it's simply sustenance."

"You're not evil?"

He chuckled and reached for her. She backed away.

"Do I look evil to you?"

Isabella blinked. He didn't appear evil. He had been kind to her. He had given her a job at a place she loved. And he was blisteringly attractive. Long black hair cascaded to his shoulders in silky waves. His eyes were the color of the summer sky. As if it had a mind of its own, her hand reached for his.

He pulled her into his arms. "I'll tell you all about us, Isabella lass, but first..." He touched his lips to hers.

She shuddered as the tip of his tongue traced the seam of her mouth and probed for entrance.

"You're so lovely, my Isabella," he whispered against her lips. "I've wanted to do this since I first laid eyes on you."

Isabella sighed and parted her lips. His tongue was gentle as he searched her mouth, and she responded without meaning to. She touched her tongue to his and began an exploration of her own. He tasted of cloves and Guinness, and some other tangy flavor that eluded her. She ran her tongue over his teeth but shrank back when she encountered the point of one fang.

The flavor she hadn't recognized? Tangy and metallic? Blood.

She pushed him away. "It was you, wasn't it? Suzanne was right."

"What?"

"You gave her to them."

"I can explain that, sweetheart. It was my nephew. I was trying to take care of him."

"They tried to rape her! You're a monster!"

"If you'll just let me explain. I never meant her any harm. I—"

Isabella could listen to no more. He *was* a monster. A demon. A drinker of blood. A vampire!

She ran up the stairs and back into the store. Then out into the sunny afternoon. Her fingers shook as they touched her lips.

She had kissed a vampire. The vampire who had been an accessory to Suzanne's near rape.

And she had *liked* it.

39

Damian followed her scent, her fear, ignoring the pain slicing through his side. She needed him. *I'm coming, mo leannan*, he called to her silently. *Hang on, I'm coming.*

His body led him to an old abandoned cottage on the outskirts of town. He stopped the bike and cased the outside of the small dwelling. Nothing unusual.

Damian heard nothing, but Suzanne's scent penetrated him.

He entered the building with stealth.

"*Voldlak*," a voice in the dark said. "I knew you'd come."

Damian shuddered. That word again. *Voldlak*. He didn't have a clue what it meant, but it spoke to him in a deep way he didn't understand. His blood boiled.

"Show yourself," he said. "Or hide in the shadows for all I care, you coward. I've come for Suzanne. Where is she?"

"Tied up at the moment, *Voldlak*. You and I have some unfinished business."

The man came forward from the shadows. The large

Blood Wolf

blond man whose fangs had been ready to pierce Suzanne's throat that first night.

"You've the right of it," Damian said. "We do have some unfinished business. The only reason you're alive is because Suzanne stopped me from killing you that night."

"Pretty sure of yourself, aren't you, *Voldlak*?"

"Why are you calling me that?"

The blond man's eyes widened, his brow wrinkled. He inhaled deeply. "You're *Voldlak,* all right."

"I'm losing my patience."

"*Voldlak*. Blood wolf." He inhaled again. "You."

Damian's ears perked up at the word "wolf." "Exactly what are you saying?"

"*Voldlak*. Blood wolf."

"Take me to Suzanne, or I'll rip your throat out right here." His irises pulsed, the first step of the change. Looking down, he noticed the hair on his forearms thickening. "Take me to her now, or I promise you'll regret it."

The blond man stared at Damian. Suddenly, another man appeared, this one with hair even paler and a strikingly beautiful face. But eyes that glowed red in the dark room. "You're losing concentration, Markus," he said. "Can't you sense it? He's beginning the change."

"I want Suzanne!" Damian roared. The wolf rose with a whoosh of his blood. He had to hold on, or he wouldn't be able to save her. He concentrated and tried to keep the bones from snapping. Once the muscles ripped and bones snapped, he would not be able to stop the animal.

"Do it, lad," the pale-haired man ordered. "Do it now!"

Markus walked toward Damian with his hands clenched into fists. "As I said, *Voldlak*, we have a score to settle."

Damian rushed into Markus and tackled him to the

ground. "Take me to Suzanne," he growled, his voice not quite human.

His muscles tightened and his strength increased. Rush. Adrenaline rush. Always the rush before the pain. He could kill this bastard with his bare hands. But not before he found Suzanne.

He wound his hands around Markus's neck, squeezed, and then pounded the blond head into the hardwood floor. "You fucking son of a bitch."

"My, my," the other man said. "I expected better from you, Markus. Dear Viveca has spoiled you rotten no doubt." He sighed. "When you want something done right, you do it yourself."

Damian looked up in time to see the pale-haired man reach toward him.

Then everything went black.

40

As much as it pained him to do so, Rex let Isabella go. He wanted to follow her, to make her understand, and then to kiss her senseless again, but that pleasure would have to wait. He still had files to search.

Hours later, he found what he was looking for. When he had opened the Lunar Eclipse twenty years previously, he had kept paper records of all his transactions. A decade later, he went paperless with computers and the Internet. In all that time, he hadn't seen either MacGowan in his shop, but he had a niggling suspicion that he had forgotten something.

He was right. In his hand, he held an invoice from nineteen years earlier. The customer was Dougal MacGowan. He had purchased a book.

A book on Lycanthropy.

41

"Och, it's about time," Dougal said aloud as his computer finally beeped its approval. Online once again after nearly four weeks, he could check his e-mail accounts and his posts. One by one, he screened them. Lunatics, mostly.

But then...

A reply to one of his posts had been sent to him via e-mail. Dougal began to read. His heart beat faster and his stomach fluttered with butterfly nerves. It couldn't be. After all this time...

And there was a cell phone number.

Dougal took a deep breath and fished his cell phone out of his pocket. Pulse racing, he punched in the numbers.

42

Suzanne lay on a cot surrounded by darkness. Markus—that was his name—hadn't fed from her. The other one, Samael, had stopped him. Said she had to be untouched.

She wanted Damian. This was all her fault. If she had made the right choice and not gone with Wade...

If she had stayed with Damian...

Her heart.

Her love.

She knew now she would never leave him. She loved him. She closed her eyes, exhausted.

Several hours later, she awoke to the aroma of chicken soup. On the table next to her cot sat a tray. Suzanne rose and realized she was famished. Dark, dank air surrounded her. She had no idea what time it was or when she had last eaten. Next to the steaming bowl of soup—ugh, she was so sick of cock-a-leekie—sat a crust of bread and a sliced apple beginning to brown. In a cup was ale of some sort. Not dark enough to be Guinness, but it smelled okay. Tangy and malty.

She had eaten about half the soup—a little watery, but not too bad—when she realized they might try to poison her. Too late now, she thought, and finished the bowl, sopping the last liquid up with the bread. Brown though it was, she ate the apple, as well, washed everything down with the ale, and then lay down again, to wait for the poisonous spasms to overtake her.

A flash of light when the door to her prison opened blinded her for an instant. She recognized the young man, Markus. "There's someone who wants to see you, wench," he said. In his hands was a white handkerchief.

"What's that for?"

"Can't have you screaming, can we?"

He pushed her down the hallway and into another room. Her gasp thudded to her stomach. Shackled to the wall and gagged, naked except for his boxers, hung Damian.

Her heart lurched, and she screamed through the gag.

"He can't get loose, lass. Those shackles are leaden. Precautions, you see. Your friend seems to have superhuman strength where you're concerned."

Suzanne struggled to free herself, but Markus held strong.

"There'll be none of that, pet." He pushed her against the wall facing Damian. "Stay there." He turned his attentions to Damian. "A pretty thing, she is. And that body." Markus whistled. "I can see why you like her so much." Markus reached out and grabbed one of Suzanne's breasts.

Damian struggled against his shackles. Suzanne tried desperately to contact him with her eyes. *Don't struggle, mo leannan. It's okay. He didn't hurt me.*

"She looks might tasty, too. Perhaps I could sample her nectar. Would you like to watch me do that?"

Blood Wolf

Suzanne clamped her legs together as Damian continued to struggle.

"She looks mighty sweet." Markus turned to Suzanne and trailed his fingers down her face and neck. "I'd like to taste every drop of juice your succulent body has to offer. And I'll start with your blood." He opened his mouth.

Suzanne watched in horror as fangs elongated and dripped with saliva.

Damian growled and pulled one of his shackles loose.

"Temper, temper," another voice said.

Markus retreated before grazing Suzanne's neck. The other man, Samael, had entered the room. Samael replaced the shackle that Damian had loosened. How? Sleight of hand? He had barely moved.

"We seem to have found our comrade's Achilles' heel, lad." Samael licked his lips, his pink tongue slithering like a serpent. "Unfortunately, he gets stronger the more you taunt him with her."

Suzanne fought the bile rising in her throat. Samael's features were chiseled and fine. But for the cloud of evil surrounding him, he would be beautiful. The stark contrast terrified her.

Suzanne's knees buckled, but Markus steadied her. "No swooning, lass. The whoreson's not worth it."

Suzanne struggled until Samael pushed Markus aside and landed a punch square on her right jaw. She cried out, but her voice was muffled by the gag. The dull thud of the punch cracked through her skin into her bone. Her teeth actually rattled.

The clank of Damian's chains echoed. From across the room, she saw his eyes swirl in anger. He broke another chain, which Samael swiftly remedied with a flick of his wrist.

Suzanne blinked.

Had Samael secured the chain without so much as a move?

Her heart pulsated under her breasts.

Darkness. She wanted to close her eyes and succumb to darkness. But air. She needed air. It was so hard to get enough into her lungs.

Hyperventilating.

She panted, trying to draw in the sweet oxygen her body craved. But it wasn't enough.

The blackness took her.

Her brain swam as she awoke, Markus shaking her violently, holding a paper bag to her face. Suzanne's mind was muddled, cloudy. "Lass, come on. I need you awake." He pushed her toward Damian until their noses nearly touched.

"Your fella hasn't been honest with you, lass," he said. "He hasn't told you what he really is."

Suzanne uttered a muffled response, pleading to Damian with her eyes. A lone tear fell from one of his hazel eyes. She had never seen a man cry before. And this one, this big, strong, amazing one, cried for her. His words filled her mind.

I'm sorry, mo leannan.

She shook her head slowly. She wanted him to know that *she* was sorry, that she didn't blame him, that she should have listened to him. That she'd never leave him again. But she couldn't reach him.

"Do you know he's a beast, lass?" Markus whispered in her ear. "A blood wolf. With a bite that can kill you without even breaking the skin?"

Suzanne shook her head. Her tummy tumbled. *No! No!* Markus was nuts.

"I can make him change for you," Markus said. "All it would take is for me to sink my teeth in that lovely white neck of yours."

Damian broke the chains around his arms again and reached for Suzanne, but Samael was faster. Within seconds, Damian was shackled again.

"His strength, you see. It isn't normal, is it?"

Suzanne's eyes widened. He did have amazing strength.

"And if taking your blood doesn't force the change, taking your pretty body sure would." Markus ripped Suzanne's blouse open and exposed her lacy beige bra.

Damian freed himself once more, only to be re-shackled by Samael's magic. His low growl resonated throughout the room, like a buzz not quite audible. Suzanne felt, more than heard it.

"Don't forget the reason we're here, lad," Samael said, his voice like smooth Scotch whiskey, hypnotic. "Not to rape the wench."

Damian's chains slackened.

"Then again," Samael continued, "she's a tasty-looking thing, is she not?"

Markus nodded, his fangs elongating. The contents of Suzanne's stomach churned violently.

"Aye, Da, that she is."

"'Twould be a shame not to take what's been so handsomely provided for us."

"Aye." Markus's green eyes darkened, and the black ring around his irises reddened.

"Take her, then, my son," Samael said. "But save a little for me."

Markus needed no further prodding. He disposed of Suzanne's shirt and plunged his sweaty hands into her jeans. She fought, but she couldn't scream. Behind her, she heard Damian struggle against the chains, but Samael's magic held him off.

Then, blessed blackness once again.

43

Time seemed not to exist. Suzanne found herself back in the darkness of the room. No one came for her, but an old-fashioned chamber pot had been provided in the corner. Several times, she awoke to find meals on a tray. She would eat, relieve herself, and then sleep again.

Fear gnawed inside her, more for Damian than for herself. For all of Markus's and Samael's threats, they hadn't yet fed from her or raped her, near as she could tell. Her bra was intact and still covered her breasts. Her lower body was still clothed, and she felt no discomfort between her legs or anywhere else.

She squeezed her eyes shut and tried to focus on Damian.
To find him.
To feel him.
She drifted into slumber again.

44

"Suzanne!"

Someone was shaking her. She opened her eyes and blinked, trying to adjust once again to the pitch darkness.

Damian. His hair was a mass of unruly waves, his eyes sunken and moist. But it was Damian.

"Get up. I'm getting you out of here."

He didn't have to say anything more. She stood up, flung herself into his arms, and burst into tears.

"Oh Damian," she cried. "I was so frightened for you. Are you hurt?"

"Nothing I can't manage. No time to talk. I have to get you out of here."

"But how?"

"Shh. Markus is no match for me. Samael left for a little while. I took the chance while I could."

"Did you kill him? Markus?"

"No. I knew that would upset you. So we have to hurry."

"My blouse is torn." It was in tatters.

"I know. But it can't be helped. It's warm out. You'll be all right."

"What time is it?"

"About half past seven in the evening."

"What day is it?"

He shook his head. "No more questions. Right now, move!" His voice reeked of authority. He meant to be obeyed.

"Damian?"

"No more, Suzanne! We must leave now. They mean to rape you when Samael returns. And I..." He stumbled over his words. "I can't allow that to happen."

Suzanne heaved, doubling over.

Damian held her firmly. "We need to go now."

Suzanne trembled as she nodded. She grabbed the sparse blanket from her cot and wrapped it around herself, hoping it would shield what her torn blouse could not.

"Come, then," Damian said, tugging at her hand.

She followed him up a dark staircase and into the living room of a small cottage, blinking as her eyes adjusted to the light. Markus lay passed out on the couch.

"What did you do to him?"

"Punched him unconscious. No more questions. Samael left, but he could be back anytime, so let's go."

Her stomach clenched as they hurried out the door. They were in the middle of nowhere, and they had no transportation.

"What now, Damian? How?"

"My bike is gone. They must have done something with it." He inhaled and let his breath out in a sharp sigh. "We'll go through the woods. I know the way back to the castle. It's longer, but it's less likely we'll be seen."

"But it will be dark soon."

Damian's eyes swirled. "I wish I knew what day it was."

"Why? What does that matter?"

He tilted his neck upward and stared at the ceiling. "Let's hurry."

45

Suzanne and Damian had been walking for half an hour, and he hadn't said one word to her. Only grunted every time she tried to talk. He kept looking at the sunset. Suzanne concentrated on the vivid shades of lavender and fuchsia. A beautiful highland sunset, it was. Under different circumstances, she would breathe deeply, relax, and enjoy it. Now, for a reason unknown to her, it made her skin crawl. The sunset seemed to bother Damian.

"Come on," he urged. "We need to move faster."

Suzanne regarded her lover. Was he *still* her lover? He hadn't tried to so much as touch her since they had left the cottage. He looked like he had lost weight. His green shirt hung on his shoulders, and his face appeared thinner.

She wanted to comfort him, but she didn't dare. She simply moved faster.

When they came to a large tree, she needed to rest. Her body was betraying her. Her stomach was clenched tight. She hadn't eaten well in God knows how many days. And her legs wobbled like jelly. "Please, Damian," she said. "I need to sit for just a minute."

"We can't."

"Please." Just a few minutes. All she needed...

He stared at her, his lips pursed and his muscles taut. But then some of the tension faded.

"Only a moment, Suzanne."

She nodded and sat down, blinking her eyes. Only a moment. Through the trees, the sun was setting. Or were there two suns? She blinked again. The sun faded...and vanished....

"Suzanne!"

Damian's voice ripped through her, rousing her from a deep sleep. He shook her. She opened her eyes. Darkness had set in.

"Suzanne. I'm sorry. I fell asleep."

"It's okay. What's the matter?"

He swallowed. "I need you to run. Run as fast as you can."

"What?"

"Away from me. Please."

The swirling irises again. His body trembled. She yearned to touch him, but something held her back. He didn't want to be touched.

"Are you cold?"

"No!" He pulled her to her feet and pushed her away from him. "Please. Go now. Run!"

Suzanne regarded Damian, bathed in the luminescent light of the full moon overhead. He remained beautiful, but something was off, and it wasn't just his lost weight.

"Damian?" Despite her trepidation, she reached for him.

He stepped back, away from her touch. Two tears streamed down his cheeks. "I know you don't love me."

"Damian—"

"Shut up!" His voice was lower, and it trembled. "I know you don't love me. I can't change that. But if you care for me at all, please do this one thing for me. I swear on my life, I'll never ask you for anything else. *Run. Now!*"

Something in his eyes made her obey. She turned and ran, twigs and leaves crunching under her feet.

46

Damian cried out as the change took him. His irises blazed with heat as they pulsed, and his vision distorted. Bones cracked, muscles stretched and contracted, tendons broke and knitted back together. Fire consumed his innards. They extended and shrank as they changed from omnivore to carnivore. Black and silver fur sprouted from his follicles, causing an uncontrollable itch. His body shook as he scratched himself. Nails narrowed and lengthened into claws, and he drew blood. His snout elongated. Tears flowed from his eyes, and he screamed as his nose broke, his septum deviated.

The worst part was the nose, even after twenty years.

No longer man, but beast, the wolf sniffed the ground. Hunger consumed him. The lust for the hunt and the kill boiled through his veins. He sniffed and caught the earthy scent of a small rabbit. His heart beat soundly as he raced toward the animal.

He stopped and perked his ears when a different aroma filled his nostrils. He inhaled.

Fresh. Musky. *Female.*
Mate.
Time to mate.
He ran as though the world were ending.

47

Suzanne stopped, doubled over, and panted. The dry heaves took her. She needed oxygen. She needed water.

A rustle from behind unnerved her, and she started to run again. Something was following her. Her bowels tightened and her side cramped in pain. But she kept running. She had promised Damian, and now it looked as though he had been right. She *was* in danger. And that danger was coming for her.

Panting and gasping, she ran as fast as her legs would go, crunching the flora beneath her feet. *Keep going,* she told herself. *Keep going.*

But a root sprang out and tripped her. Having landed on her face, she moved to get up. The rustling behind her was louder now. Whatever stalked her was not far behind.

"Damn it, get up!" she said aloud.

As she rose, an animal hurled itself through the air onto her and flattened her on her back.

Her breath came in short puffy gasps as her heart

pounded. The animal's claws pressed into her abdomen, knocked the wind out of her, and sent icy pain into her bowels. She gulped and nearly vomited, and then she looked up at her attacker.

A wolf.

Black with silver markings.

Very large.

Her pulse raced. She opened her mouth and screamed.

The wolf growled at her, pawing the blanket wrapped around her chest. His fangs dripped with saliva. And his eyes, a curious color of brownish green, swirled as he stared into hers.

Curious.

And recognizable.

Damian.

They were Damian's eyes.

Blood wolf.

Samael had said Damian was a blood wolf. She shuddered under the weight of his lupine body.

A werewolf?

The full moon shone brightly, bathing them in its veiling light.

Could it be?

"Damian?"

No response.

The animal continued to paw at her and growl, his eyes a blazing mass of swirling green.

Suzanne gasped, groping the thick night air for oxygen.

"Damian, I know it's you. Please don't hurt me."

His growl was low and angry. Primal. She had but one shot. She had to reach him—if indeed it was him—or die.

"Damian. Don't do this. It's me, *mo leannan*. Suzanne."

He ripped the blanket off her with his claws.

"You don't want to hurt me. I know you don't." Tears streamed down her cheeks as her heart opened. "I trust you, Damian. You won't hurt me."

The wolf cocked his head and gazed at her silently.

"I love you, Damian." Suzanne reached out a trembling hand and rubbed his flank. "You. Only you."

The wolf released her, backed off, and sat a few feet away.

She rose to a sit to look at him. "It *is* you."

She approached him with hesitancy, sat next to him, and tentatively touched his dog-like face. His fur was soft, like the fleece of her blanket, and it tickled her shaking fingers.

"My God, you're beautiful."

She jumped when he growled again. Something was different, though. It wasn't coming from his throat, but from his stomach.

"They starved you, didn't they?" She stood up. "I'll find you something to eat."

He whimpered. She didn't know how, but she understood that he needed to go himself. That he had to kill an animal to eat.

"All right, then. Go. I'll be fine. But I don't want to see it, okay?"

He cocked his head.

She needed to add something else, but she wasn't sure how. She trusted him with her life. But she wasn't sure about the lives of others. Yet. She spoke hesitantly. "Damian. Please don't hurt any people."

He trotted off into the darkness.

An hour later, he returned to her and lay down beside her. She wrapped her arms in his silky fur and slept.

48

"What are you doing here?" Isabella glared at Rex Donnelly. "It's not even sunrise."

"Isabella, this is my sister, Viveca." Rex motioned to the stunning woman who stood beside him.

Raven hair framed an oval face and fell to her shoulders in cascading curls. Her skin was the color of moonlight, and her lips the incandescent crimson of a ripe cherry. Her eyes, though, outshone the rest. The color of a clear emerald and lashed with ebony, they held sadness. And pain.

"Rex has told me much of you," Viveca said. "I'm sorry I haven't come into the store to meet you before now. I've been —" She sighed. "Very busy, I'm afraid." She held out a pale hand.

Shaking, Isabella touched her hand to Viveca's perfectly manicured red-tipped fingers.

"Isabella," Rex said. "I know you're upset with me, and I cannot blame you. I acted foolishly. But we need to talk. Please. It's important."

"Rex, my cousin and her boyfriend are missing. They've been gone for over forty-eight hours, and—"

He cut her off. "I know. That's why we're here."

"Dougal's been out day and night, and I only came home to get some much-needed sleep last night."

"Dougal will not find them, sweetheart."

Isabella's heart leaped at the endearment, but she ignored it and pursed her lips.

"I had a hunch my nephew, Markus, might be involved, and I've been searching as well, with no luck. But this morning..."

"What?" Isabella nearly shouted. "What happened this morning?"

"Er, well, Viveca here..."

"I got a visit from Markus's father, my dear."

Isabella's gaze met the other woman's. While Isabella prided herself on her ability to read people—it was part of being a witch—what she found in Viveca's striking eyes startled her. Pain and sorrow, yes, but also regret. And love.

"May we come in?" Viveca said. "The sun is rising, and our kind don't do well in sunlight."

Isabella didn't want to invite them in, but her curiosity had been peaked. She also had no desire to see two people burst into flames on her front porch. For the first time, she noticed both Rex and Viveca wore long sleeves and pants, despite the summer heat.

"Forgive my ill manners," Isabella said. "Please, come in."

"Markus's father and I were never actually married," Viveca said, "but he was the love of my life, and I of his."

"So then, what happened?"

"It doesn't matter," she said. "What matters is that he and Markus have your cousin and the young MacGowan."

"Why? Why would they want to hurt Suzanne?"

"It's not Suzanne they want, sweetheart," Rex said. "It's Damian."

Isabella's widened her eyes. "What?"

"You see, Markus thinks Damian is—" He cleared his throat and paced the hallway. "Markus thinks Damian is a blood wolf, Isabella."

"What's a blood wolf?"

"A werewolf, in layman's terms," Rex said. "But a different kind of werewolf than you've probably heard of. I always thought they were a myth, but evidently Markus thinks otherwise."

Isabella's knees buckled, but Rex caught her. Her heart jumped at his touch, but again, she ignored the feeling.

"He means to kill Damian, Isabella."

"But Merlina's book says that vampires—"

"Aren't killers. She's right. And frankly, if Damian *is* a blood wolf, Markus won't be any match for him. Samael, on the other hand, is another matter."

"Samael?"

"Markus's father," Rex said.

"Another vampire?" Isabella shook her head. "If Damian can handle Markus, why couldn't he handle his father?"

"Because, my dear, the father of my son is not a vampire." Viveca laid a hand on Isabella's forearm. "He's a demon."

Isabella wasn't aware she had fallen to the floor until Rex lifted her into his arms and carried her down the hallway and into the parlor. He set her gently on a sofa.

"Are you all right, sweetheart?" He caressed her forearm lightly.

Viveca sat on the other side of Isabella. "'Tis my curse to love a demon, child. I didn't know what he was when we made Markus together. When I found out, I sent him away, and he visits me only in my dreams, and only then when he's near Padraig. He came to me early this morning."

Chills cut through Isabella's skin.

"He said he had been with our son. He didn't have to say more. I knew, then, as only a mother can, that my son and his father were involved in your cousin's and young Damian's disappearance."

"S-So," Isabella stammered, "what do we do now?"

"I can find Samael, child," Viveca said. "He's in my heart, my soul. And he's near." She stifled a sob. "The others, including my son, are not safe."

"Then let's go."

"Isabella," Rex said softly. "I don't want you to come along."

"Are you crazy? Of course I'm coming. Why else would you come here?"

"It was my idea," Viveca said. "I felt you had a right to know what's going on."

"But—"

"Please." Rex's cerulean eyes melded to hers. "I know I've no right to ask this of you, but I can't have you put in danger. I couldn't bear it. Will you trust me, lass? Will you trust me to bring them home to you?"

"But the sun is rising. How?"

He smiled gently, his eyes kind. "Are you worried for me, sweetheart?"

"No. Of course not."

"We've the best sunblock available, made for our kind. And glasses with UV protection. And you'll note we've covered as much skin as we can with our clothing."

"I—"

"Will you trust me, Isabella?" He caught her tear with his forefinger and pressed it to his lips.

Her heart nearly stopped.

"Please."

She slowly nodded. "I trust you."

She had no other choice.

49

Suzanne awoke as the sun rose and cast its rays through the thick foliage of the woods. Damian lay next to her, naked, in human form. She drew her fingers over the muscle of his chest and traced the hair around his nipples, down his stomach, and then laced her fingers through the thick black curls between his legs. His cock grew instantly, and his eyes opened.

"Morning," she said.

"My love, I'm so sorry."

"For what?"

"For nearly—"

"But you didn't. You didn't want to kill me."

"No, no. I wouldn't have killed you. That wasn't what I was after."

"Oh?"

"I wanted to mate with you."

"Oh." Suzanne fought her gag reflex. "I'm not sure what to say to that."

"It likely wouldn't have worked anyway. No matter. You're

safe from that now. You got through to me. No one's been able to until now."

She stroked his cheek. "Why didn't you tell me?"

"Because you'd have run away from me like a rat from a tomcat."

"No."

"Aye."

Suzanne sighed. "You're right."

"I'm not going to lie to you. I know little about this, er, condition."

"What about Dougal? Is he one too?"

"No. He's not my natural da. He found me when I was a wee bairn."

"Oh. Goodness." She was at a loss for words. "This is all starting to make an eerie sort of sense. Isabella found Merlina's magical documents. Evidently, Padraig is home to a host of, shall we say, *interesting* people."

"If you mean vampires, you're correct, as you've no doubt figured out. The man Markus is a vampire."

"Clearly. What of Samael? I heard Markus call him Da."

Damian shook his head. "I'm not sure what he is, but he's not a vamp. My best guess is a demon."

Suzanne nodded, unwilling to explore the subject of Markus and Samael any further.

"*Mo leannan*," Damian said.

"Yes?"

"Did you mean it?"

"Mean what?"

"When you said you loved me."

She warmed as fierce emotion surged though her body. "Yes, Damian. I meant it."

"All of me?"

"Yes. All of you."

"The man and the beast?"

She nodded. "But I don't want to..."

He chuckled softly. "I know. Nor do I. Don't worry. I won't try it again. Don't ask me how I know, but I do."

She laughed nervously. "You haven't steered me wrong yet."

"And I never will." He traced her lips with his finger. "As much as it will pain me, I want you to go back to America."

"What? You're kidding, right?"

"No. You're not safe with me."

"Of course I am. You didn't hurt me last night."

"That's not what I mean." Damian cleared his throat and looked away. "Markus took you because of me. It was me he wanted. He nearly raped you. He—" Damian choked on his words. "He would have if you hadn't fainted."

"I wondered why he didn't."

"I took care of it."

"How?"

"It's not important. What's important is that you stay safe, and you'll be safe in America."

"Too bad. I'm not going."

"Yes, you are."

"Always domineering, aren't you, Damian MacGowan? Don't you know by now that I'm not fond of following orders?"

Damian shook his head. "Your safety is the most important thing."

She shook her head. "Think again." She walked into his arms and embraced him, running her hands up and down his back. What? "Turn around, Damian."

"No."

"You know I'll see it sooner or later." She walked around and looked at his back. The beautiful wolf was scarred with lashings. The sores had oozed during the night, and dirt and leaves stuck to the wounds. Suzanne's hand whipped to her mouth as her stomach threatened to empty. "That's how you kept them from raping me. You let them beat you."

He nodded slowly. "Aye."

"Oh, my sweet love." She kissed his lips. "Which one of them did this to you?"

"Markus."

"The other one held you in your chains? I couldn't understand how he did that."

"He's a demon, love. And no, he didn't hold me. Part of the bargain for your safety was that I offer no resistance."

"My God." She swallowed to hold back a heave.

"So you see why you need to leave, Suzanne. I can't risk them taking you again."

"I can't believe you did this for me." She choked back a sob. "But I'm safe with you. You got me out of there."

"But there's no guarantee they won't try to take you again because of me."

"And there's no guarantee the sun will rise tomorrow, either." She took both of his hands in her own. "When I went with Wade the other day, it took me all of five minutes to realize I'd made the wrong decision. That I wanted to go back to you. That I loved you." She brought one of his hands to her lips and brushed them over his knuckles. "I'm so sorry, Damian. If I'd listened to you, I wouldn't have been in this mess. So you did protect me. I was the one who was wrong. And I'll always trust your judgment from now on."

"You'd really stay with me? Here in Padraig?"

"Here or anywhere else you want to go, my love."

He grabbed her and nearly threw her into the air. "I promise you none will harm you as long as I live."

"You've proven that."

He kissed her hard. Then, "Thank God. I couldn't bear to lose you. I don't think I could go on." He smoothed her tangled mass of hair. "I want to love you, *mo leannan*."

"Nothing stopping you that I can see."

"The wolf still runs through me. I'm not sure I could be... gentle with you."

"I trust you."

"I'm not sure I trust myself. That first night, when I found you behind the Pit with the vamps, it was the first night after the full moon. The beast was still in me. That's why I was so persistent."

"But you didn't force me, Damian. You're a man, not a beast. A very kind, gentle man."

"*Mo leannan*, I wanted—"

"I know what you wanted. But you respected my wishes. Looking back, I think I fell in love with you that night. When you held me, comforted me, and let me sleep in your arms. It was clear you wanted me." She smiled. "I felt it against my thigh all night. But you resisted. For me."

"Do you want to know when I fell in love with you?"

"When?"

"When you looked upon my body and trusted me to look upon yours. It was then I knew, not only were you mine, but mine to love."

"Oh, Damian." She crushed her body to his. "Make love to me. You don't have to be gentle. I love all of you. The man and the beast."

"I want you more than you can imagine, but I will not hurt you. Never, while I breathe, will you be hurt again."

"Then love me, Damian. Just love me."

He ripped her jeans off, raised his body over hers, and thrust into her. He wasn't gentle. He pounded into her body with a feral passion, groaning her name as he pumped. No kissing, no caressing. Just raw, untamed joining.

"Take me, Suzanne," he roared. "Take all of me."

He thrust and thrust, and Suzanne's hips rose to meet him, her thighs bruising under his attack. The pounding crossed the barrier from pleasure into pain, but still she rode with him, reaching and reaching, and when the climax took her, she grabbed his bottom and forced him farther into her. "Come with me, Damian," she said. "Come with me."

"Aye," he groaned, plunging into her hard. "Aye, take me, *mo leannan*. Make me yours."

She felt every spasm of his release as he gave himself to her—body, heart, and soul.

They lay together afterward, not talking, simply being.

Suzanne trailed her fingers over Damian's naked chest and relished his heavy rasps as she traced his nipples, and then his boyish chuckle as she scraped her nails down his belly to his navel, tickling him. She knew his body so intimately, what pleased him. How to make him quiver under her touch.

Finally, she spoke. "What will we do for clothes for you?"

"They're not far from here. I managed to get most of them off before the change. And you'll wear my shirt. I can't let you walk around like that." His eyes raked over her bare breasts. "Though keeping you naked certainly is an enticing thought." He leered at her, and she swatted him, smiling.

"We'll go get the clothes, and then—"

"Then I take you home, *mo leannan*. Our home. Where I can take care of you and keep you safe. We should go. Markus won't stay out forever, and I've no idea when the other one will come back."

They walked the short distance to Damian's clothes and dressed to begin the long walk back to the castle.

"Damian," she said, "will you help me with my—" Chills raced along her spine. Something was wrong. She turned. "Damian?"

Where had he gone? He had been behind her buttoning his jeans a minute ago.

"Damian?"

50

"He's with me da," said the low voice she remembered. Markus stepped from behind a tree. "I've nothing against you, lass, but you've caused an awful lot of trouble, haven't you?"

Suzanne trembled as the vampire approached her. "Where did he take Damian?"

"Da is madder than ever. And trust me, lass, you don't want to be around my da when he's in a bad mood."

"Please. You've got to help me. I know you're not a"—she nearly choked—"a *bad* guy. Please. Let him go."

"'It's no longer up to me. In the meantime, I think you owe me a little taste of your sweet blood." His fangs grew as he leaned down toward her neck.

Suzanne let out a piercing scream and squeezed her eyes shut as his teeth scratched her skin.

"That'll be enough, Markus," a feminine voice said.

Suzanne opened her eyes, still squinting. A beautiful dark-haired woman stood facing Markus, and next to her was Rex Donnelly from the bookshop in Padraig.

"Christ," Markus said, "what are you two doing here?"

"You don't want to hurt the lass, Markus," Rex said. "The wolf will hunt you down if you touch her."

"Da's taking care of him."

"Not for long," the woman said. "Sam! Samael del Morte, you show yourself this instant!"

Damian appeared in the leaden chains, Samael beside him.

"Vivi?" Samael said tentatively.

"It's me, Sam. You don't want to hurt that lad."

"Ah, but I do. I've a score to settle for my son."

"No." The woman approached Samael and touched his face. His red eyes turned to a woodsy green. "Let him go."

"I... I..." His features softened, and his forest gaze raked over the woman who touched him. "Only for you, sweet Vivi."

The chains around Damian disintegrated, and Suzanne ran into his arms.

Samael traced the lines of the woman's face with his long, elegant fingers. He trailed over her eyebrows, the tips of her eyelashes, her nose, and at last, her red mouth. "It's been over a century since your lips last touched mine, Vivi, and not a moment has gone by since then that I haven't dreamed of this moment."

Suzanne's breath hitched in her throat as Samael's lips joined with the woman's. Passion cut through the air, so thick it was palpable. A pink aura, intertwined with threads of black, surrounded the couple.

"What is that?" Suzanne asked.

Damian shook his head.

"It's passion," Rex said. "Visible passion. Only a demon can produce it. Can't you feel it?"

Damian hugged Suzanne's body closer to his, and his arousal pressed against her belly. Her nipples tightened. Her anger diffused, and happier emotion sliced through her.

"My Vivi," Samael said when the woman finally broke the kiss.

"Leave them alone, Sam," she said. "For me."

"Aye. For you."

"And Markus, Sam."

"He needs his da."

"He needs me more, Sam. Leave him to me."

"I could never deny you anything, Vivi. I'll stay away. But not forever."

The woman nodded. "That will do for now."

"Good-bye, my love." He lifted her hand to his lips. "Until you dream again."

He vanished.

Rex turned to Damian and sniffed. "You're *Voldlak*, all right. I never would have believed it."

"What are you talking about?" Suzanne demanded.

"It's an old legend, lass." He arched his eyebrows at Damian. "You mean you haven't told her?"

"I've told her all I know, Donnelly."

"Which is?"

"Which is nothing. I change at the full moon. My da's not my natural da. He found me as a wee bairn. What the bloody hell is a *Voldlak*?"

"The *Voldlak*, lad, are an ancient race of werewolves. Blood wolves, they call themselves. And their bite is so lethal that it can kill a vampire or a human without even breaking the skin."

Suzanne shuddered and eased away from Damian. She

had slept next to his wolf last night. His saliva had dripped on her.

"Suzanne—" Damian began.

"I'm sorry, it's just—"

"Christ. Now you don't trust me again."

"It's not that."

"Then what is it? Don't you think I know what you're doing? You're looking for evidence of my bite."

"No."

"'Tis an old legend, lad," the woman said. "Most of it is probably myth and nothing more." She inhaled. "But you are *Voldlak*. Any vampire would know your scent. It's bred into us."

"I've nothing against any of you, except him." He gestured to Markus.

"He won't bother you or your lassie again," Rex said. "You have my word on that."

"You'll understand if your word doesn't mean jack to me, won't you, *friend*?"

"We're not friends, lad," Rex said. "We never will be. Our blood prevents it. But I care about your lassie here, because I care about her cousin. I'll not see her harmed. And harming you would harm her."

"Damian," Suzanne said, "I think you can trust him. He just saved your life."

"No, *she* saved my life." He nodded to the woman. "And you are?"

"Rex's sister, Viveca. Markus is my son."

"Och," Damian said. "This gets better and better, doesn't it?"

"Let's just get home, Damian," Suzanne said. "The walk'll do us both some good."

"Are you kidding me? This is just fine with everyone?" Damian pointed at Markus. "He's just going to get away with kidnapping Suzanne and nearly killing me? And what about the demon?"

"Evil is its own punishment," Viveca said.

"Not while I'm standing. Where do I find him?"

"Damian." Suzanne trailed her fingers gently up his arm. "You can't defeat him. He's a demon. You've been under his power. I'm amazed he let us get away the first time."

"I'm not that amazed," Viveca said. "He saw your love. He felt it in his heart. Yes, he does have a heart. And it ignited a tiny memory of his love for me and mine for him."

Damian rolled his eyes. They swirled with rage. "How touching. Then I'll settle for him." He turned to Markus.

Markus growled, his fangs elongating.

"Damn it all!" Viveca marched toward her son. "Stop it, for God's sake."

"Mum—"

"He'll kick your arse, and your da won't be here to save it this time." She grabbed Markus's arm. "You're damned lucky you're still standing."

Suzanne closed her eyes and inhaled. When she opened them, she met Damian's swirling gaze. "Please. I just want to go home."

Damian let out a long breath of air. "All right. Let's go."

"You're welcome to come with us," Rex said. "Viveca and I have an auto."

"No thanks," Damian said. "Suzanne and I will walk."

"Thank you for coming," she said to Rex and Viveca. "Both of you." She motioned to Damian. "Don't you want to—"

"No," he said, taking her hand. "Let's go."

51

"Thank God!" Isabella pulled Suzanne into a hug when she and Damian returned to the castle. "Rex came by and told us you were okay."

"Aye, you both gave us quite a scare," Dougal said, embracing his son. "And you have a visitor." He pulled Damian into the living parlor.

Suzanne followed. Seated on the wingback chairs were a man and a woman.

"Meet Rohricht Telikov and his wife, Elena," Dougal said.

The man rose to greet him.

Damian's heart jumped. A face gazed at him. A striking face.

A familiar face.

52

Rohricht pulled Damian into a deep hug. "I would never have believed it," he said.

Damian broke away, confused. When he inhaled, he noticed a faint smoky aroma, like nutmeg laced with patchouli.

"What is that?" he asked. "That scent? It's..." He inhaled again. He felt as though he couldn't get enough of it.

"It's the scent of mates," Rohricht said. "It's the scent of Elena and me. It's coming from you as well. You and your lady there." He motioned to Suzanne. "You can't smell it on yourself, but any other wolf can smell it on you. And on your mate. It's a warning to others that she's been marked."

"You're a—"

"Yes, I'm like you. I'm your uncle."

"My uncle?"

"Your father was my older brother, Aleksander. We called him Sasha."

"But how?"

"DNA testing can prove it easily enough, boy. But that

would only be for your benefit. Your scent is enough for me. That and the fact that you're a dead ringer for Sasha. Except the eyes. They must have come from your mother."

"Damian?" Suzanne took his hand.

"Sit, lad," Dougal said. "It's a miracle, it is. Rohricht here came upon one of our posts."

Damian sat down on a sofa and pulled Suzanne down beside him. "I don't know what to say."

"Don't say anything," Dougal said. "Just listen."

He nodded, and Rohricht began to speak.

"We're an ancient race of wolf shifters, known in legend as *Voldlak*. It comes from the Russian word *volkodlak*."

"You were right, Da," Damian said.

Dougal grinned.

"Most of us are in Russia, though a few have scattered here and there."

"So I'm Russian, then?"

"Half. Your mother was Scottish."

"Can you tell me anything about her?"

"Yes, but not much. Sasha came to Scotland thirty odd years ago. He was young at the time, not more than nineteen, and he didn't expect to find his mate so soon. Most of us don't mate until we're in our thirties, but it can happen."

"Mate? You mentioned that before. What does it mean, exactly?"

"Well, boy, let me ask you this. When you met your lady, there, did you know right away that she was yours?"

"Aye."

"That's what it means. We, like the wolves of the wild, mate for life. There is only one female for each male, and the male knows when he finds her. By her scent.

"We were plentiful millennia ago. Many different types of

people inhabited the planet. But as humans propagated, the old races died out. We didn't, but we evolved. Our males began to take human women as mates, and the females they bore were human, not wolf."

"Then there aren't any—"

"There aren't any female shifters in our clans. No. All males take human mates now. Only in recent years have we learned the scientific reason for this. It seems the gene for shifting is carried on the Y chromosome. Our scientists and philosophers think we evolved in this way to preserve our race among the influx of humans. There were few wolf women, but plenty of human ones."

"But only one for each of us?"

"Yes."

"Then if the wolf gene is carried on the Y chromosome, any male children I father will be wolves."

"Yes. And females will be human."

"So we are human, then? Just with a different gene?"

"Our DNA is indistinguishable, but there are a few differences. For one, we can only impregnate our true mates."

Damian scoffed. "Then all those years of condoms?"

"Were unnecessary. At least for contraception. But we are susceptible to most human diseases, so you were smart to use them."

"Uh, Damian," Suzanne said, "just how many years and how many condoms were there?"

"Not many, *mo leannan*. And none that mattered."

"He speaks the truth," Rohricht said. "When a wolf finds his mate, the feelings are indescribable."

"The vampire said something about my bite being lethal," Damian said.

"Our bite, when we're in wolf form, is lethal. But only to

vampires. Not to humans and not to other wolves. The legend says it can kill without breaking the skin, but I've not heard of that actually happening. Our saliva does burn vampire skin, though, and if it gets into their blood stream, it will result in a nasty infection, which can end in death, but doesn't always."

"Can you tell me more about my da? My biological da?"

"He was to be the Alpha of our pack. But he died over thirty years ago. So when my father passed on, it fell to me. But you, as his natural son, are the true Alpha."

Damian widened his eyes. He was the Alpha? He wasn't sure he wanted that. He didn't want to leave Dougal. He didn't want to leave Scotland.

"When Sasha came to Scotland all those years ago, he met and fell in love with a young maiden of sixteen. For a wolf to find his mate at such a young age is unusual, though not wholly unheard of. He swept her off her feet, and they had a couple of wonderful months together, but when he told her the truth about himself, she fled."

"She was young," Suzanne said.

"She was." Rohricht nodded. "And as you no doubt know, the truth about us is a lot to take all at once. Sasha followed her for several months, trying to convince her to stay with him, but she'd have no part of it. Finally, he needed to return to Russia to sit at our father's side for the grand council that happens annually. It was then that he told us about his Maggie.

"He returned to Scotland a few months later. She had died at the hands of vampires. Vampires who had no doubt smelled him on her."

"They smelled him?" Damian stood. "Markus said he smelled me. But why now? I've lived here all my life."

"Our scent doesn't ripen until we mate," Rohricht said. "When did he first notice you?"

"The night I went after Suzanne." Damian sat back down, nodding. "It's all making sense now. But what happened to my da?"

"He died himself within a year."

"Was he ill?" Suzanne asked.

"No, dear. He was fine. But once a wolf finds his mate, he cannot live without her. Wolves and their mates will not live long without each other."

"Oh!" Suzanne's clasped her hand to her mouth.

"My mother didn't abandon me." Damian's heart ached for his mother's fate, but the veil of her love surrounded him. "She was protecting me from vampires when she left me in the alley."

"Of course she didn't abandon you. And neither did your father." Rohricht smiled. "Tell me, when did you first experience the change?"

"I was fifteen."

"That's about the right age. Usually in the middle of puberty."

"Aye."

"And you respond to the call of the moon?"

"The full moon. Aye."

"Have you ever changed at another time?"

"No. Though there have been times when I thought I would, but I was able to control it."

"The lunar pull here in this little town is strong," Rohricht said. "I felt it as soon as we got here. The full moon will begin to wane tonight."

"Aye."

"The good news, boy, is that you no longer need be slave to the moon. I can teach you to control the change."

Damian shot off the sofa. "You can?"

"I imagine it's been difficult, with no one to guide you. The first change is painful and frightening."

"Aye. It was. Still is."

"You can learn to control the change. If you change frequently during the month, at your own will, the lunar pull will not control you. You will learn to keep your human consciousness during the change as well. Shall we start?"

"Now?"

"Can you think of a better time? The moon will call to you come nightfall."

"Let's do it, then."

53

"He's the best thing in my life," the red-haired Elena said to Suzanne and Isabella. "I know I couldn't live without him now."

The three women worked in the kitchen, preparing dinner, while the men, including Dougal, worked outside. Suzanne had briefed Elena and Isabella on the earlier events.

"Did you consider leaving him when you found out?" Suzanne asked.

"Only briefly. I knew there would never be another for me. Isn't it the same with you?"

"Yes, it is," Suzanne said. "Looking back, I fell in love with him the first night I met him, though at the time, I denied it."

"Even though we mates don't possess wolf blood, I've found, from my own experiences and from speaking with others, that the attraction is just as strong for us as it is for them. It's a lucky woman to be mated to a wolf." She lowered her voice. "They're fantastic lovers."

"Okay, now I'm jealous," Isabella said, laughing.

"I think Rohr is going to want Damian to come to Russia to meet the clan," Elena continued. "He'll be able to train him better there."

"Wow." Suzanne let out a sharp breath. "I don't know if he'll leave Scotland. Or Dougal."

"What of you?"

"I'll go with him wherever he decides to go."

"Oh, Suze, I was so hoping to have you here," Isabella said.

"Wolves are pack animals," Elena said. "They're happiest living close together."

Suzanne sighed. "I guess we'll wait and see what Damian decides. He's a writer, so his work can go anywhere."

"I hope you do come to Russia," Elena said. "You and I will be great friends."

"I think we would be. And Bell, you can come to visit. Hey, maybe one of the wolves will claim you!"

"I..." Isabella's cheeks reddened.

"Unless there's someone here you have your eye on," Suzanne teased, "like a certain handsome bookshop owner."

"Suze, he's a vampire."

"You're not going to get all prejudiced on me now, are you? I'm mated to a werewolf!"

"I know, but after what he did, what his nephew did..."

"If I'm not holding a grudge, why should you?"

"Why *aren't* you holding a grudge, Suze?"

"I suppose I should be. I can't describe it. That passion between the demon and Viveca. It...*changed* something inside of me. I wish you had been there to experience it. Besides, Damian's holding enough of one for both of us."

"Well, I don't know."

"Just keep an open mind, Bell. That's my best advice."

Isabella smiled, and Suzanne's heart filled with warmth. She would miss her cousin if she went to Russia. But her place was at Damian's side.

54

Later, after dinner but before nightfall, Damian cornered Suzanne in a small alcove on the top floor of the castle and pressed his lips to hers. "Thank you for the delicious dinner. I'll never starve with you as my mate."

"I'll take great care of you," she said, laughing.

"I know you will. And we have some things to discuss."

"Like?"

"Like, how would you like to see Russia?"

Suzanne's shoulders slumped a little, but she forced a smile. "I'll go wherever you go, Damian."

"I know you will. And I thank you for that. I love you." He kissed her hard. "I need to go, to meet the others, and to learn more about my kind. But I've already told Rohr that I won't take his place as Alpha. My place is here, in this castle, with my da. My real da. And with you. Scotland is my home."

"Oh, Damian!" Suzanne threw her arms around his neck and sprinkled kisses all over his lips and cheeks. "I'm so glad we'll be coming back here!"

"I couldn't live anywhere else, *mo leannan*. But there is something we need to take care of before we go."

"What's that?"

"You need to marry me."

"Is that a proposal?"

"Aye. Would you do me the honor of becoming my wife?"

"Yes, yes, yes!" She kissed his mouth. "I will marry you, Damian MacGowan. My sweet, handsome wolf."

He grabbed her and pushed her against the wall, lifting her cotton skirt as he fumbled with his jeans.

When he was inside her, both of them gasping, he said, "We need to talk about those pills of yours, *mo leannan*. How do you feel about cubs?"

"I love cubs," she rasped and then soared into the fading sun, taking her wolf with her.

THE END

A NOTE FROM HELEN

Dear Reader,

Thank you for reading *Blood Wolf*. If you want to find out about my current backlist and future releases, please visit my website, like my Facebook page, and join my mailing list. If you're a fan, please join my Facebook street team (Hardt & Soul) to help spread the word about my books. I regularly do awesome giveaways for my street team members.

If you enjoyed the story, please take the time to leave a review. I welcome all feedback.

I wish you all the best!

Helen

Sign up for my newsletter here:

http://www.helenhardt.com/signup

ABOUT THE AUTHOR

#1 *New York Times*, #1 *USA Today*, and #1 *Wall Street Journal* bestselling author Helen Hardt's passion for the written word began with the books her mother read to her at bedtime. She wrote her first story at age six and hasn't stopped since. In addition to being an award-winning author of romantic fiction, she's a mother, an attorney, a black belt in Taekwondo, a grammar geek, an appreciator of fine red wine, and a lover of Ben and Jerry's ice cream. She writes from her home in Colorado, where she lives with her family. Helen loves to hear from readers.

Please sign up for her newsletter here:
http://www.helenhardt.com/signup
Visit her here:
http://www.helenhardt.com